WE'RE ON OUR WAY TO GERMANY!

Haydn Middleton

SCHOLASTIC

Scholastic Children's Books,
Commonwealth House, 1-19 New Oxford Street,
London, WC1A 1NU, UK
a division of Scholastic Ltd
London ~ New York ~ Toronto ~ Sydney ~ Auckland
Mexico City ~ New Delhi ~ Hong Kong

First published in the UK by Scholastic Ltd, 2000

ISBN 0 439 01455 7

Typeset by TW Typesetting, Midsomer Norton, Somerset
Printed by Bath Press, Bath, England

1 2 3 4 5 6 7 8 9 10

1

It was 9:30 am on a wet Monday in November. An even bigger host than usual of TV, radio and newspaper reporters was camped outside Ash Acre, the crumbling home of Castle Albion FC. Not for the first time that season, Albion was a club in crisis. Why? Two days before, the blue-and-white-hooped wonders had been knocked out of the FA Cup in only the second round.

Now all kinds of rumours were flying about. Manager Benny Webb was going to get the boot! Half the squad was being put up for transfer! Gazza was being signed on loan! No player would be allowed to open another super-market for the rest of the season! Almost anything was possible at Ash Acre – where for the past seven months mega-rich schoolboy James "Jimbo" Prince, the computer wizard, had been chairman. Little Jimbo had big, big plans for the Albion. He wanted to put the club up among the game's élite and it wasn't in his nature to hang about.

Suddenly the media scrum came alive as a silver stretch-limo with smoked windows purred to a halt outside the main entrance. At once the great sleek car was engulfed by men with microphones and notepads. Who could be inside? *Was* it Gazza? Or some new foreign player maybe? Everyone kept saying that what Albion desperately needed was a glamorous big-name star from overseas.

The car's arrival caused a stir further down the street as well. That was where a horde of players' agents, marketing executives and would-be sponsors were parked up in their own motors – all awaiting the chance to tempt any member of Albion's squad with money-spinning offers. They dashed at the limo too.

The uniformed chauffeur got out and opened the rear door. There was a brief pause, then the tallest man that many in the crowd had ever seen appeared. He wore an ankle-length raincoat with the collar turned up, and a kind of cowboy hat pulled down over his eyes. Those eyes were hidden by shades, and most of the rest of his face was covered by a dark bushy beard.

"Well it's definitely not Gazza," breathed one reporter. "Way too thin!"

"Is it someone Spanish?" whispered an agent. "Or Latvian? Or Afghanistani?"

They called out greetings in a dozen of the

languages spoken nowadays by players at English clubs. But the towering newcomer responded to none. In fact he ignored everyone as he headed, a little unsteadily, towards the club entrance. Then he ducked his head, and stepped inside the badly dilapidated ground.

So many phones were going in the offices, so many faxes coming through, and so many tickets being sold, that no one spotted the tall guy. Looking even less certain on his feet, he opened a door on to a long, dingy corridor. When he got to the end of it he paused outside a peeling blue door that said Home Team. From behind it came the sound of somebody going ballistic. Not one of the words was clear. It was more like a constant gargling roar, with just the occasional pause for breath. Benny Webb was reading his players the riot act.

"You can't go in there, mate," called someone from a narrower corridor running off to the left. "Players and officials only."

The tall guy turned to see who had spoken. There were three people crouching down near the wall – a man holding a camcorder, another holding a boom mike, and a woman scribbling busily on a clipboard. They had become a familiar trio around Ash Acre. Back in August, Chairman Prince had agreed to let them make a fly-on-the-wall TV documentary about the whole of Albion's season.

"The manager will have your guts for garters if you go in," the man with the mike went on. "He's had ours already, even though our contracts say that we *can* film in there." He raised his eyebrows. "Mr Webb is *not* a happy camper."

The tall guy nodded, then turned back to the door, opened it and went inside.

"What the...?" gasped the white-bearded figure in a sheepskin coat who was standing on one of the benches – Mr Benny Webb, manager. "Who the...?"

But before he could grab a bag of footballs and start hurling them one by one at the intruder, a very odd thing happened.

The tall guy reached up and began to unbutton his long coat from the neck down. Meanwhile, a second pair of hands appeared below, and began to unbutton simultaneously from the hem upwards. There was a bizarre moment when they met at the middle button – and in a flurry of fingers it wouldn't come undone. But at last the coat flew open. And there inside were two schoolboys in Albion kit, one perched precariously on the shoulders of the other! But these weren't just any school kids. Both of them were solid-gold soccer superstars – and for almost a year they'd been the undisputed kings of this footballing castle.

"Luke Green!" grinned club skipper Gaffer Mann.

"Frederick Dulac!" cried midfielders Narris Phiz and Michael "Half-Fat" Milkes.

"Sorry we're late, Boss," Luke said to Benny, clambering off his best mate's shoulders and pulling off the false beard. "Our French lesson overran. And we thought this disguise would be the best way to get straight into the ground."

"Avoid the media and merchandising vultures," Frederick added coolly, taking his shades back from Luke and sitting down.

"OK, OK," sighed Benny. "I was wondering where you lads had got to. And, my oh my, did we miss you on Saturday afternoon, Luke! *Diabolical*, it was." Suddenly his ever-anxious face became even more worried-looking. "Hey, there's not gonna be a problem about you playing on Wednesday night, is there?"

"No, Boss," Luke smiled, as he pulled on his trademark trainers, but he knew why Benny was worried. Luke wasn't always able to slip past his football-hating mum to get to games. For although he had become a legend all over the football-loving world, *she* still didn't know he even played – which could cause major headaches. "My stepdad's got it sorted."

"Well that's a major relief," said Benny. "Without you, son – and Frederick here – we're gonna go down by a cricket score." As Luke sat, Benny glared at the other players who were ranged round the cramped little dressing-room's walls. "I've said it before and I'll say it again: the rest of you should be ashamed that we depend so much on a pair of kids to keep gettin' us out of jail. Now – where was I before they came in?"

Several players scratched their heads. Then big-bellied goalie "Madman" Mort (the living answer to that eternal question: Who's Eaten All the Pies?) beamed broadly and put up his hand. "You were saying we were the biggest, most disgraceful bunch of dimwits it's ever been your misfortune to manage, Boss."

"Ah yes," said Benny. "Cheers, Morty." Then, as everyone winced, he took a deep breath and carried on ranting from the exact point where he'd left off.

2

Benny went on and on. He hadn't liked being knocked out of the cup. Not one bit. Nor had the fans. Nor had anyone else who was in any way associated with the club.

Now this might seem odd. Albion were in Division Three of the Nationwide League – and most Division Three clubs don't expect to get much further than the FA Cup Second Round. Castle Albion *did*. In fact, just one season before, they had battled through to the third round. Then the fourth. Then the fifth. Incredibly they had made the quarter-finals. Stupendously they reached the semis. And finally, miraculously, on a glorious day in May which no true football lover would ever forget, they beat Man United at Wembley to *win* the fabulous trophy!

They had turned the football world upside down. And even now Luke found himself wondering if it had all just been a dream. But it really did happen. It was as real as the hair in

Desmond Lynam's moustache. Albion won the cup! Which was always going to be a hard act to follow. But, during pre-season training, Benny had told his team he wanted them to get to the semis this season – at least. And so it came to pass that, after scraping past Leyton Orient in the first round, Albion were drawn against Unibond League minnows Leek Town at home.

No games in modern football are easy. But just try telling that to Leek. They came to Ash Acre, they saw an Albion side in total disarray – and they conquered them to the tune of two goals to one. Albion, the holders, were out!

Benny picked on player after player, savagely listing their errors. Plump goalie Madman; wingbacks Craig Edwards and Dennis Meldrum; stopper and skipper Gaffer Mann; midfielders Phiz, Milkes, former YTS lad Chrissie Pick and Luke's stand-in, the club's player-physio Terry Vaudeville; striker Carl Davey.

Only two members of the defeated team got away without a verbal pasting. One was Luke's mate, the bottom half of the tall guy – "Cool" Frederick Dulac, the classy sweeper. "If it hadn't been for Fred, they'd have had two more," Benny muttered. "And he scored as well. None of the rest of you even got *close*!"

But the eleventh player from Saturday's game didn't get any kind of mention. This was the player wearing the number ten shirt in honour of his all-time idol, Pelé: the small, spindly boy with glasses who was no older than school-age stars Luke and Cool F, and was currently taking a call on his mobile by the communal bath, watched over by a burly minder in a penguin suit and black bow-tie.

"It's no good, Benny," this lad piped, suddenly making for the door ahead of his minder. "I can't get a proper signal in here. I'll have to go out on the pitch. It's the stadium contractors. You carry on without me for a minute." He eyed Benny sharply through his specs. "But you're right to be disgusted about Saturday. It was a disgrace to be knocked out by a team that none of us had even *heard* of before! If we don't get our act together soon, heads will roll!"

With that, he was gone. And even though Benny Webb hadn't mentioned *his* contribution to the Leek defeat, all the players now put that right in an enormous chorus: "He's so bad it's unbelievable!" "My Granny's got a better shot than him, and she's been dead for five years!" "He couldn't be any worse if you tied his legs together!" "He can't kick, he can't run, he can hardly see!"

"Lads! *Lads!*" groaned Benny. He'd heard all this before – way too many times. "That's enough! You know this situation as well as I do. It's not what any of us would have wanted, but there it is. We're stuck with it."

And the reason they were stuck with it was that Albion's most useless player ever was *also* Albion's chairman. The kid in the specs was none other than James Prince, teenage supremo of Majestic Software. And whereas Luke and Frederick were good enough to be regularly approached by Celtic, Juventus and Barcelona, Albion's third youngster wouldn't have got a game against a wall.

"What you've all got to remember," Benny went on, "is that without Mr Prince, this club wouldn't exist now. He was everybody's hero when he took control last May and paid off all our debts."

"Yeah," groaned Dennis Meldrum, "but was it worth it? Every time he plays he's worth a two-goal start to the opposition. He's ruining everything."

Benny shook his big shaggy head. "I've got to come clean there," he said. "When he said he wanted to play, as part of the deal, I thought he'd be much too busy ever to pull on a shirt..."

"Or at least realize how rubbish he was," Carl Davey continued, "then hang up his boots after his first game."

"But no," said Craig Edwards. "He's only missed about five matches."

"All the ones we've won," pointed out Chrissie Pick.

"And it's all because of him that we're

sixteenth in the league," Half-Fat concluded, "And out of the FA Cup. I mean, who scores *two* own goals in a cup-tie? And then he's got the nerve to say 'Heads will roll'!" Luke saw Benny wince at that. No manager is ever more than a few bad results away from the axe. Poor old Ben knew full well that the first head on the block would be his own.

"Well, that's as maybe," said Terry, the veteran player-physio. "But the boss wasn't wrong before. We were lucky to come second on Saturday. Only Cool F did the business. I reckon the rest of us get infected by JP. His uselessness sort of rubs off."

"All right, all right," concluded Benny, "you've had your say now. But it's like I've been telling you on the quiet all season: the other ten of you have got to give 125% every game – just to make up for young Jimbo. *That's* why I keep having such a go at you all. You're just not giving me that extra twenty-five per cent!"

"I dunno about giving stuff to *you*," muttered Carl Davey. "Someone ought to give Jimbo something. Like five months' worth of flu. Or a nice broken leg."

"You can't get near him, though, can you?" shaven-headed Chrissie Pick put in, taking this suggestion quite seriously. "Not with all his minders."

"Now then, now then!" Terry V shouted. "We

don't want any talk like that." He glanced away. "But *if* – in a training session – someone was to go in on him a little bit too enthusiastically, say… Well, accidents do happen, don't they?"

The room fell silent. All the players looked first at Terry, then at Benny who was pretending not to have heard, then at each other, and slowly the same grin spread over each of their faces. Terry winked. In the trickiest situations, you could always rely on TV for a plan. This one was certainly worth a try.

"OK," Benny resumed. "Let's put Saturday behind us, get out on that pitch and train like there's no tomorrow for – er – the day after tomorrow's game."

Everyone jumped up and rushed to the door, whooping and hollering. As Madman Mort passed Benny he clapped him on the shoulder. "There *is* one good thing about going out of the FA Cup so early, Boss," he grinned.

"Oh yeah? What's that, then?"

"*Now we can concentrate on the UEFA Cup!*" chorused Narris, Dennis and Gaffer over their shoulders in reply.

And they did have a point. Because on Wednesday night at Ash Acre stadium, Castle Albion – the English cup-holders – were playing in the third round first-leg of one of Europe's premier tournaments. Against Bayern Munich!

"Oh please!" Benny gasped, shivering at the

mere thought of the task ahead. "From Leek Town to Bayern Munich. Who ever said football was a funny game?"

3

No one got a chance to nobble James Prince that morning. Even before Benny got everyone doing warm-up laps, Luke and the other players watched the skinny little chairman throw a monstrous wobbly on his mobile.

"That's *not* good enough! I *won't* accept that!" he screeched, hopping up and down. "No *way* will I accept yet another postponement of the opening!"

Luke and Frederick exchanged wide-eyed looks. They knew JP didn't live in the real world. Anyone who aimed to put Castle Albion on a par with Liverpool and Lazio had his head in the clouds. And his plan to build a brand-new, state-of-the-art stadium to be opened in time for Christmas was just plain crazy. Didn't he *know* that builders needed that long just to drink their tea?

In the end he hurled the mobile at his nearby heavy – who caught it, magnificently, in one hand – and stomped across the muddy grass to

Benny. "It's no good," he told the boss. "I'll have to go up there and deal with this. They're making a fuss about the retractable roof. God, they're like *children*! But look, just make do without me. I'm feeling pretty fit and sharp anyway."

By then the minder had radioed for the chauffeur to back his limo into the area behind the West End goal. JP knock-kneed across to it. "I'll see you before the Bayern game," he called over his shoulder before disappearing into the ultra-luxurious motor. "Have to miss training tomorrow. Trip to New York."

So that was that. Short of the player-chairman coming a cropper over the Atlantic in his private jet, he would be in the starting line-up versus Munich.

"Some you lose, some you lose," murmured Carl as all the first-teamers set off on their first lap of the pitch. But, without Jimbo to mess everything up, the morning went extremely well. Fast running, no one pulling out of the exercises, a mistake-free rehearsal of all the set-pieces, then a confidence-boosting practice match against the apprentices from Albion's new soccer academy.

It all went better than any session Luke could remember. Not that he'd been to many. His headmistress, a lifelong Albion fan, let him out of school for only one training-session per week. But since this was such a special week, she was letting him out for two. He couldn't grumble. The head had dreamed up all sorts of "school activities" to put Luke's mum off the scent while he travelled to games in places like Hull, Cardiff and Carlisle. But even she hadn't managed to get him to Malta or Turkey for the away legs of Albion's two UEFA Cup ties so far. And it didn't seem likely that Luke would be visiting Munich either.

To be fair, it was pretty amazing that *anyone* from Albion was going to Munich. They'd won their first round home-leg against Malta's Sliema Wanderers three-one, with the chairman safely away on business and Luke scoring twice. The away leg was another story. Luke out, Princey in; Albion going down three-nil. But then news broke that the Maltesers had used an unregistered player as a late sub. Sliema were disqualified; Albion found themselves in the hat for Round Two – where they were paired with Turkey's awesome Fenerbahce.

This time Luke didn't even make the home leg. It was his mum and stepdad's wedding anniversary, and she absolutely insisted that all three of them should go out to a Thai restaurant to celebrate. It turned into a double whammy for Luke. He went down with a dicky tummy from all the spices, and with Jimbo giving away a goal-line free kick in the fifth minute, Albion went down nil-two.

There was more Turkish Delight at the away leg. The Pride of Istanbul won by another two clear goals and, once again, Albion departed the UEFA Cup. But, once again, the next morning they found themselves back in it.

This time, Albion's opponents were kicked out of the competition after some home fans went ape seconds before the final whistle. Thinking it was all over, they invaded the pitch to celebrate. The ref tried to clear them off but high spirits took over, and somehow one of the goals got dismantled – so ending any attempt to finish the match. No club can survive in a European competition when that happens. (But no one quite knew afterwards how exactly Terry V got among the pitch invaders, in Fenerbahce colours. Or how – as Midweek Sports Special replays suggested – he seemed to be the main culprit tearing down the posts.)

"All right, Luke?" asked a deep voice as everyone trooped off the pitch after training. Luke turned to find big Ruel Bibbo. "Stayed on your feet most of the time today, then?" Smiling, he nodded at Luke's trusty mud-spattered trainers. The young "Studless Sensation" had never mastered the art of playing in boots.

Luke smiled back. Old Ruel, one of the first black strikers ever to play for England, had kept turning out for Albion right up to the FA Cup Final. After that he'd finally called it a day – only to be re-employed at once as chief executive of Albion's new soccer academy, a pet scheme of Princey's.

"I think you could just nick a result on Wednesday," Ruel said. "Remember what happened the *last* time Bayern played an English side." How could anyone forget? Champions League Final, 1999. Bayern one goal ahead with two minutes to go. Then Man U struck twice to whisk the trophy right out of their hands. "They won't be taking anything for granted. Wish *I* was playing."

"We *all* wish you were," Luke replied. "We've never replaced you. Carl has to do it all up front. Benny only puts James alongside him to keep him a safe distance away from our own goal. We just don't have enough firepower."

Ruel nodded his grey-haired head. "I know what you're saying. But don't get the wrong impression. There *is* a striker on the way. Trust me on that."

Luke stopped in his tracks. If he'd heard that once since August – from Benny, from Terry, from Ruel – he'd heard it a thousand times. But what did it *mean*? Whenever he asked, each of the three would just wink and look embarrassed.

" 'On the way', you always say. 'On the way'. But when's this mystery man actually going to *get* here?"

Ruel looked shifty. "Well, as things stand,

that's a bit of an open question. But all will be revealed in due course. And I'm telling you: it'll be worth the wait. Believe me, Luke, English football has never seen anything *like* this guy!"

4

Luke didn't usually get nervous before big games. But on Tuesday night he did start to feel the odd jitter. *Bayern Munich!* he kept thinking – awestruck – at dinner. OK, so Man U had pipped them in 1999. But they'd once *won* the European Cup three times in a row. This was *not* a team to mess with.

And his stepdad Rodney hadn't helped by drooling over all the Bayern greats from the past: Franz Beckenbauer, Gerd Müller, Karl-Heinz Rummenigge, Lothar Matthäus... This wasn't going to be like playing Sliema Wanderers or Fenerbahce. Little Albion had a full-scale Goliath in their way now.

"What *is* the matter with you, Luke?" his mum sniped at him when she caught him in a daze over the washing-up. "You're hardly here with us tonight. And thanks to Rodney, you're not going to be here with me tomorrow night, either."

"Ah yes," Rodney cut in as he picked up

another plate to dry. "I'm glad you remembered about the meeting, dear. But we'll only be out from seven till ten."

Luke's mum shook her head. "Well, I don't know, I've never heard of a group like this before. 'Neighbourhood Birdwatch'? And you seem to be having so *many* meetings. Why can you never have one here?"

"Oh," said Rodney quickly, his glasses flashing in panic, "you don't want to be bothered with that, dear. The wives always have to lay on tea and biscuits. And you've got enough on your plate already, what with…" He paused, unable to think of a way to go on. "And besides, we're all so *boring*, us birdwatchers."

"I'd have to agree with that," she snorted back. "I'm surprised that *you*'ve taken such an interest though, Luke. I never thought birds were your thing."

"They didn't used to be," Luke told her after a glance at Rodney. "But they are now. I … I'm always on the lookout for a bird. Nowadays."

"Hmmm," said his mum, picking up the week's TV guide. "I suppose I'll just have to make do with television again…"

"Oh, why bother with that, dear?" Rodney intervened, whipping the booklet away. "There's never anything worth watching on a Wednesday. I'll rent you out a video. Just leave it to me. Something with lots of gardens in it.

You do love gardens, don't you? Gardens and gardening? Nothing better!"

Luke's toes curled inside his trainers. He knew how important this was. His mum could never watch TV without flipping impatiently from channel to channel. And on one of them, tomorrow night, Albion v Bayern was being shown live. If she caught sight of so much as a footballer's kneecap, she would flip away again in disgust. But what if she *recognized* that kneecap? What if she heard the commentator saying something like, "Luke Green, the Albion playmaker, is calling all the shots in midfield at the moment"?

She would not be best pleased.

She would make one of James Prince's tantrums look like a *Blue Peter* presenter telling you all about his holidays.

As far as she was concerned, Luke had not kicked a football – professionally or otherwise – since she had forbidden it outright nearly a year before. It would not be good for Luke's health, or Rodney's, if she now found out how wrong she'd been.

At 9:45 Luke went up to his room. He was cleaning his teeth when the phone rang. Luckily Rodney answered. Moments later Luke heard him shout, "Luke, it's for you. Your – ah – *schoolfriend*: Cutlet. Could you take it up there?"

Cutlet! With a mouth still full of toothpaste, Luke rushed out on to the landing and lifted the receiver. This was no friend from school. "Cutlet" was Rodney's code-name for someone who had no business in any place of education. This was Neil Veal, players' agent. *Luke*'s agent – quite unbeknownst to his mum.

"*Ciao*, Luke," oozed a voice as oily as the sea at a British coastal resort. "Glad I caught you. Just want to touch base. Quick update: bit of movement on the *Lukewarm* front..."

"I told you never to call me at home," hissed Luke. "If Mum twigs, I've had it!"

"No worries there, Lukey. Just slam down if she starts sniffing around. I'll cut to the chase. The *Lukewarm* people have a new model for you to test-drive. Vastly improved. Brand-new design. If you could be at Ash Acre ten minutes early on Wednesday night, you can give it a trial. No probs? Ace! See you there."

Luke was still struggling to speak as the line went dead. Vealy wasn't the easiest guy to talk to, either by phone or in person. He represented half a dozen members of the Albion side, and although he did pull off a lot of deals, they weren't always quite what his clients wanted.

Cool Frederick was happy enough. Veal had negotiated a sleek new Adidas boot for him, the *Fredator*. But then he'd dropped Craig and Dennis in it by securing them a £100,000 publishing deal for a jointly-penned novel about babes 'n' soccer: *He's Scored!* – without checking first whether either of them could actually write.

And now, for the young Studless Sensation himself, there was the *Lukewarm*.

Luke had never liked the sound of this. Who really needed an "internally-heated training shoe"? And he would have to wear the blessed things too, every time he played! Oh well, maybe the new model would just catch fire before he could try it on, like the last one. And at least Veal was sticking to their agreement to involve him in deals that showed him only from the neck down – he just couldn't risk letting his mum see his face up on some billboard. (Which had led certain jokers at the club to refer to him occasionally as the Headless Hero.)

But, as Luke's head hit the pillow that night, he wasn't giving much thought to footwear. *"Bayern Munich, Bayern Munich, Bayern Munich,"* he kept on breathing out loud – as if just by saying the name he could make the mighty German club seem a little bit less unbeatable.

"That's enough praying in there," snapped his mum, as she passed his doorway on the way to her room. "Whatever you're asking for, I'm sure God's heard you by now. Get to sleep, Luke. And no dreaming about football!"

5

At 7:05 on Wednesday evening the little streets around Ash Acre were so densely packed that even a football-mad sardine would have felt the pinch. The ground could hold only 13,000 people – most of them standing on cracked, weed-covered terraces – and at least twice that many were wanting to get in.

James Prince, standing in kit and boots just inside the main entrance, looked out at the rain-soaked multitude and shook his head. "You see," he fumed to Luke, Rodney and anyone else who would listen. "*That*'s why we need a purpose-built all-seater stadium near the motorway with acres of parking space. This place is medieval. I was ashamed to welcome our German guests to it."

Ah, the German guests. Luke had watched them arriving. It was like seeing a footballing hall of fame take shape before his very eyes.

Stefan Effenberg, the proud skipper; Oliver Kahn, the acrobatic keeper; Lothar Matthäus, the old campaigner who had seen and done it all; Lizarazu, the French World-Cup-winner, Tarnat, Jeremies, Elber the Brazilian... Then, last off the coach, the thrilling young Paraguayan striker Roque Santa Cruz (or Santa Claus, as Benny kept calling him by mistake at team briefings).

Luke also caught a glimpse of club president Franz Beckenbauer giving a TV interview in perfect English. Now there *was* a star. Rodney had recalled him playing out of his skin in the World Cup Final of 1966 which England won. But the original "Becks" hadn't let that bother him. In 1974 he'd captained his country to World Cup victory, and then, sixteen years later, he was their manager when they won the ultimate prize again.

"So, Franz," ITV's Gary Newbon was asking him. "How do you fancy your chances here tonight?"

"Oh," smiled the man they called "The Kaiser", "if we can do half as well as Leek Town did on Saturday, I will be happy with that!"

"Luke! *Luke!*" hissed a voice behind him in the madly-busy foyer. Luke turned to see a spotty concoction of hair gel and Raybans poking out of the gents toilet. Neil Veal! He always popped up where you least expected him.

"We'll have to do the trainer test in here," he explained, beckoning to the boy wonder. "No room anywhere else. Won't take a sec. Brill!"

Luke said goodbye to Rodney as Vealy held the door back. Inside, two frizzy-haired men in white lab-coats were hunched over the single washbasin. Luke had met these guys twice already. Dutch, they were. Or maybe Iraqi. Veal never seemed entirely sure. He called them "inventors", but Luke seriously doubted whether they'd ever invented anything to do with feet before.

"Hello!" said the first, turning. "Headless Hero!" These were the only words in English that he knew. Which was three more than his accomplice, who now turned too. In both hands he was holding up a white trainer which seemed to be trailing a thin grey line of smoke. The *Lukewarm Mark Two*!

"Slip it on, Luke, mate," Veal said, tapping his client's shoulder. "Look at it! Just the job for a jog on a chilly winter morning! Monster!"

Luke laughed out loud and backed off. It *was* smoke. Lots of it. The red-faced guy holding the thing was desperately trying to stop himself from coughing. "You've got to be kidding," Luke told them all, reaching for the door handle. "I want to *play* my socks off – not burn them off!"

"Minor design fault," Vealo protested feebly, but Luke was already leaving. "Just teething probs. We'll get back to you! And hey – enjoy the match!"

There were now only ten minutes to kick-off. Luke wormed his way past all the officials, former players, former players' wives, celebrity glory supporters, the fly-on-the-wall unit and assorted hangers-on, to get to the dressing room. The moment he entered, an enormous anguished roar went up from Carl Davey. Luke grinned. The striker was only going through his regular pre-match ritual. Before every game, Craig Edwards hurled a pineapple, hard, against Carl's backside. Carl reckoned it made him more likely to score. Something had to.

Benny booted the squashed fruit into a corner and clapped his hands. "All right, lads!" he boomed. "Let's talk."

Everyone shut up. Benny's team talks could strip paint off the hot-water pipes. Tonight, however, he had a nervy look on his face.

"Well this is it, lads," he began. "You're up against the United Nations here tonight. Brazilian, French, Paraguayan. And what have we got to hit them back with...? The best of British, that's what! I want to see some real bulldog spirit out there on the park. I wanna hear you lot *barking*! Got me? I want to see with my own eyes what put the Great into Great Britain!" His eyes were starting to flash now. "Forget about all those fiascos in the league. Forget about Leek Town." He lifted his bearded chin. "Just get out there and show them Bayernets who's boss!"

A deeper hush settled over all the players. Luke and Frederick exchanged puzzled glances. Was that it? What about tactics and strategy? How about individual dos and don'ts for each and every one of them? Or detailed breakdowns of what to expect from every player in the Bayern squad? And what about poor old Narris Phiz, from Trinidad, who wasn't even British anyway?

"Oh, and one other thing," Benny remembered. He turned with a grim look to where James Prince sat, wedged in between two minders. "James – I want you to stay *well* forward, right? Always give us an attacking option. You *never* need to come back further than the halfway line. Got that?"

"Never!" confirmed Terry V. "Absolutely not *ever*!" Gaffer added, while everyone else nodded their heads. It was the only way they had of stopping JP from scoring own goals or conceding free kicks in dreadfully dangerous places.

"OK, Boss," Jimbo replied, jutting out his little jaw. "Fine, if you think that's the best way to use me. I'm glad you rate my attacking capabilities so highly. And what better game than this for me to hit my first goal for Albion?"

Luke ducked his head to hide a smile. So did pretty well everyone else. You had to hand it to old Jimbo. He couldn't kick a ball to save his life, but he *thought* he was a world-beater. Attitude? This boy had it in spades!

"So get out there now, you pack of British bulldogs," Benny went on. And the whole squad – plus two minders – leapt to their feet, hungry for action. "And remember – BARK!"

6

Luke lined up in the tunnel next to Lothar Matthäus – the man who had lifted the World Cup trophy in 1990! He was getting on a bit now but he still looked super-fit.

"Hey, Studless Sensation!" he grinned across at Luke, and playfully punched his shoulder. "We've heard all about *you* in my country! You should come and play for one of our clubs, *ja*? We have heating in the dressing rooms there!"

Luke grinned back. They had heating at Ash Acre too – but Terry usually made sure it didn't get switched on in the away-team dressing room. Then, to a huge roar from the mostly sodden 13,000, both teams raced out on to the pitch.

What a buzz! The whole shoddy, wondrous place was *steaming* with Euro-fever. TV cameras bristled among the ancient floodlight pylons and rusty sheets of lead roofing. The wind-up stadium clock still showed 4:48 (the time when the whistle had blown at Wembley and Albion won the FA Cup). And there at the uncovered Town End, hundreds of bare-chested Munich fans were singing fit to burst and letting off fireworks into the cold, drizzly night.

As both teams kicked in, the long-suffering stadium announcer fought a losing battle with his tannoy system to give out the players' names. Halfway through the home list, the speakers sputtered into silence. But the hardcore Albion fans on the South Side terrace, led by Supporters Club Chairman Rocky Mitford, helped out by yelling all the rest. Then they announced the world-famous Bayern side too, player by player, to enormous applause from the Town End.

"Good job we haven't got to have the national anthems," Chrissie Pick shouted to Luke, nodding up at the dodgiest speakers in the Nationwide League. "You'd have thought old Jimbo could have got a PA system sorted, wouldn't you?"

Luke shrugged and smiled. Princey had always declared he "wasn't going to throw money at the club". If his throwing was anything like his kicking, he would have missed by a mile anyway. He certainly hadn't shelled out on new players for the European campaign – saying he preferred to stick by the guys who had won the FA Cup to "see if they could do it on the bigger stage".

He was still sinking millions into his new Majestic Stadium, though. It was going to be a shopping and hotel complex as well as a sports arena. (JP hadn't got where he was today without spotting big business opportunities.) That was all very well, but sometimes Luke wished he'd just tarted up Ash Acre a bit.

"I see *your* fan club's out in force tonight," he said to Chrissie, pointing at the North Stand. As soon as slaphead Chrissie turned to look, a horde of *very* attractive young women screeched and squealed as if he was a cross between Joe Fiennes and Jamie Redknapp. Some of them held up a banner saying:

Chrissie Pick – The Bald Bombshell!

Smaller, individual ones said:

Pick *Me*! Pick *Me*!

"Tell me about it," sighed Chrissie. "I had that Kate Moss on the phone this afternoon *begging* me for tickets. I wish she'd give it a rest." In August, Vealy had wangled the Pickman a catwalk job as a model for Versace. Ever since then he'd been harassed by love-sick super-vixens. ("It's not as great as you might think," Luke heard him tell Narris one morning. "I haven't been out with *one* who likes The Prodigy yet. Or chips. All they want to do is not eat.")

Then the ref blew for the toss-up – and Gaffer called right, so Albion got to aim at the away end for the first forty-five. That was just how they liked it. It meant they would be kicking towards their own fans in the game's crucial second period, with the rabid, jampacked West End *sucking* the ball goalwards. You've heard about fan-assisted ovens. Here you got fan-assisted goals.

The crowd noise when Bayern kicked off was spine-tingling. So was Luke's first sighting of the visitors' crisp, speedy inter-passing. They all seemed to be covering the ground twice as fast as any Albion player. Three times in the first ten minutes they forced corners. From the second, a Santa Cruz header beat Madman at the near post, only for Dennis to flykick off the line. From the third, a phenomenal twenty-five-yard volley from Effenberg grazed the woodwork.

Benny was up off his bench already, wind-milling his arms and screaming instructions that no one in an Albion shirt would have understood even if they'd heard him. But the tide of German attacks was irresistible. For the next fifteen minutes, it didn't do Bayern justice to say that it was one-way traffic: from Luke's angle, it was like facing the wrong way on a six-lane motorway – *all* of them fast lanes. The only way to avoid being mown down was to step on to the hard shoulder – and watch Madman make a string of glorious saves.

The pressure just wouldn't ease up. Mätthaus

had two shots, Scholl two, Elber two, Jancker three... Obviously the Germans were going all out for a priceless away goal (since – as everyone knows – away goals count double in European two-legged ties). But in the twenty-sixth minute, something unexpected happened. After Madman had intercepted yet another cross from Lizarazu, he didn't simply punt it upfield and wait for it to come back. This time, Cool Frederick backpedalled to the left-hand touchline and called for the ball.

Madman hurled it to him, Cool F trapped it so deftly that he was able to push it to Santa Cruz's left, then run round him to the right to collect it.

At once Basler rushed up to close him down, but Frederick nutmegged him, ran on a short distance, then swung a pinpoint crossfield ball to Luke on the right touchline, ten yards inside the German half. Luke hardly had time to look up before two midfielders converged on him. But having waited so long to get the ball in a decent position, he wasn't about to give it away.

With a feint to the left, then another to the right, he left both Bayernets for dead. The Albion faithful could only grunt, gobsmacked, to see their side attacking after so long under the cosh. Then foghorn-voiced Rocky Mitford snapped them all out of it with a rousing cry of *"Go Lukey! Go Lukey!"*

Lukey obliged, taking out Kuffour with an

outrageous dummy, then floating over a delicious cross to Kahn's far post. *"Go Carly! Go Carly!"* bellowed the Albion thousands as the Pineapple Poacher leapt with the keeper and got his head to it first. Carl's looping header wasn't quite on target. Instead the ball plopped into the goalmouth mud and slowly trickled along the six-yard line.

The Bayern defence was all over the place – caught completely napping. Not one man in a grey shirt with the *Opel* logo was close enough to hoof it away. Not as close, that was, as one player in blue-and-white hoops who suddenly darted forward. A player who, up to that point, hadn't had a single kick or header. His sole contribution had been to stray offside nine times.

Princey!

This time no whistle blew. The semi-naked German supporters behind the gaping Bayern goal froze. Even Rocky and the Southsiders gaped in silent wonder. And in that sudden split-second of eerie silence, James Prince – businessman, chairman, player, nerd – took one more stride towards his destiny.

7

But for a footballer of Princey's calibre, even a simple stride forward could be a complicated business. With the bobbling ball still two steps away from him, he swung his right foot but seemed to forget that, in order to move in a forward direction, he had to lift his left foot as well.

Luke winced. Thirteen thousand Brits and Germans caught their breath in horror. Most male bodies aren't built to do the splits. Jimbo Prince's certainly wasn't. His scream of agony as he scissored down into the mud would ring in Luke's head for a long time afterwards. And he wouldn't quickly forget the sight of JP's right boot-sole finally making contact with the ball – and pushing it harmlessly past the far post for a goal-kick.

The stadium came alive again. As the player-chairman writhed on the deck, and the ref made stretcher signals to the dug-out, Terry V took a good while to trot across to the patient. Luke and half a dozen others gathered round as Terry poked and prodded away. Luke had never been quite sure how deep Tel's medical knowledge went. His treatment for just about every on-field injury seemed to be a quick squirt from the sponge, followed by advice to "Run it off, mate".

"Ooh," he was saying this time though, as Princey's noise died down, "this looks pretty serious to me. I think we'll have to pull you off, old son."

"Yeah, yeah, right!" chorused all the watching Albion players.

But no.

"Just get me back on my feet," Jimbo panted. "I think I can carry on."

"No, surely! You can't! *No!*" groaned the sympathetic players – who seemed to be trying harder to force JP back down than to help him up. But this was one determined young man. Soon he was upright again, pulling a few faces, but ready to leap back into the fray. "Hey!" he cried at Cool F. "Did I score?"

The next nineteen minutes never hit the same heights and depths as that first twenty-six. Bayern put on the brakes after so nearly being caught out. And although Luke and Cool F worked some good openings for Albion, there simply wasn't anyone up front to finish off the job. Jimbo never touched it again. And as for

Carl Davey's first touch, he could have been *playing* with a pineapple.

In the dressing room at half-time Benny ranted and raved, but Luke heard none of the usual fire in his voice. Most of the players seemed a bit saggy too. In a way, that was crazy. For here they were, holding their own against the cream of the Bundesliga, but still they were down in the mouth! Luke thought he understood, though. However well they played, however loudly they barked, JP was always going to be there to foul it all up in some way.

"You sure you wanna risk another half, James?" Benny asked just before they left again for the pitch. "We've got that crunch game at Cheltenham on Saturday. I'd hate to have to lose you for that one."

"No, Boss. I'm completely back to normal now," piped little Princey, slapping the insides of his thighs. So many eyebrows went up, you could almost hear the hairs rustling. "And you know what? I think we can have these!" He stood and tapped the wall that divided them off from the shivery Bayern dressing room. "They're nothing special. Come on, guys, let's hear that bulldog spirit now! Woof woof, right? Woof woof *woof*! Woof woof woof *woof WOOF*!"

Cool F frowned at Luke as Jimbo went on and on. "Barking," he mouthed.

Bayern started the second half just as awesomely as they'd started the first. Santa Cruz, the young Paraguayan, seemed to be on a one-man mission to wrap up the tie. Twice he brought the very best out of Madman with wickedly dipping volleys – and if any lesser player than Cool F had been marking him, he would surely have had a hat-trick. Jancker, too, was giving Gaffer a torrid second period. And each time Matthäus surged forward, Luke heard every individual Southsider roar in a panic:

"Pick him up! Shut him down! *Stop* him!"

Yet, by hook or by crook, Albion kept their goal intact. They never looked like nicking one themselves, but as long as they didn't concede at home, they would still have a shout in the return leg in two weeks' time.

Then, right out of nowhere, in the eighty-second minute, everything changed.

It started when Craig took a quick throw-in over by the dug-outs. Benny was so close to him, screaming and waving, that he could almost have taken the throw himself. And Bayern's trainer, Ottmar Hitzfeld, was up and shouting too.

Craig's throw was good and long, down the touchline. Carl had already set off on a great run towards the corner flag. Even so, Babbel looked to have him covered and was favourite to get to the ball first. But, for a second, the rugged defender was distracted by Hitzfeld's shouts. Carl edged in front of him and, just before he reached the ball, Babbel lunged in from behind to get there first.

It looked a lot worse than it was. He only clipped Carl's ankle, but the Albion man went down like a sack of old pineapples and the crowd bayed for blood. The ref rushed up, yellow-carded the fouler, and signalled a free kick. And that was a job for Albion's dead-ball specialist: the Studless Sensation.

Luke trotted over to where a rapidly-recovered Carl had already placed the ball. He felt a tingle of anticipation pass from the crowd right through him. Luke knew this tingle. He'd had it before: a goal was in the air. The deadlock-breaker. Resettling the ball, he glanced up into the crowded Bayern box.

He was forty yards out. Too far for a shot, even for him. But a curling far-post cross could wreak pure havoc. Benny obviously thought the same thing. He'd waved Gaffer and Cool F forward. Craig had crept up on the far flank too. There was never going to be a better chance to take the lead.

Albion had to give it everything they'd got. But with everyone up, *someone* had to hang back – in case Bayern suddenly broke. Dennis was just over halfway, keeping an eye on Santa Cruz. But one-on-one was asking for trouble.

"Back!" Benny blared at Narris. "Get back to the centre spot! We gotta have cover!"

The crowd was making too much noise, though. Narris didn't see or hear. Yet the player just in front of him did. Jimbo. Winking at Benny, he gave him a thumbs-up, then back-pedalled to the halfway line, falling over only once.

Oh well, thought Luke as the ref blew his whistle – at least he's out of harm's way for a moment. Then in he ran, made perfect contact, and sent the ball spinning high *across* the box – over everybody's startled heads. Everybody except Cool F. Because, as Luke ran in, he had peeled away from Effenberg and dropped ten yards deeper. Now he was racing in again. And, as Luke's precision cross dropped down, he met it with a volley so fierce that the leather screamed for mercy.

No one saw the ball flash past from Frederick's boot. Kahn didn't even turn as it arrowed goalwards but not, as luck would have it, straight into the net. Instead, it zapped against the crossbar, so hard that it rocketed back out over everyone's heads again – this time towards the Albion end.

Santa Cruz was first to react. Springing away from Dennis, he met the ball on its second bounce and flicked it over both their heads. His turn was too whippet-quick for Dennis, who slipped and fell in trying to match him for pace. But the pricey Paraguayan had flicked it just a little too far: over the halfway line, where James Prince was still standing sentry.

For a split-second, the ball was *way* closer to JP than to Santa Cruz. But Luke watched, aghast, as the player-chairman hesitated to go for it. And he knew just why. All those instructions *never* to venture into his own half! Surely he could see this was different, though? Surely he could see he *had* to go for it now? He did, but too late. For Santa, Christmas had come early. He powered past Jimbo, took two delicate touches to get to the edge of the Albion box and, as Madman rushed out, he chipped him – to perfection.

Castle Albion nil, Bayern Munich one! The bare-breasted ones went bananas. Everyone else in the stadium gazed, slack-jawed, from Kahn's still-shuddering crossbar to Princey, to the messy pyramid of celebrating Munich footballers.

There was no way back for Albion now. Not that night. They laid siege to the German goal, but it wasn't to be. They huffed and they puffed but the house built in the Bundesliga would not be blown down. When the ref blew for full-time, Luke sank to his knees. So near and yet so far.

Bayern had boldly gone where Leek Town

had gone before. They had that priceless away goal too. Football! It could be the world's cruellest game.

8

Luke still hadn't fully recovered by Friday evening. He kept seeing Benny's shell-shocked face at his post-match interview. The guy had hardly been able to put two words together – until Gary Newbon's last question: "You're still looking lightweight up front, Benny – no new signings on the horizon, then?"

"Er – well," Benny blinked and swallowed hard. "I wouldn't say that."

"Really? But anyone you sign now won't be eligible for the away leg, right? You're way past the UEFA deadline for new players."

Now Benny blushed on six million TV sets. "Er – I wouldn't say that either."

"So what exactly have you got up your sleeve, then?" Gary pressed.

Then poor old preoccupied Benny actually peered down his sheepskin coat-sleeve – before Terry came up and steered him away to the dressing room. What *was* this all about? Luke wondered all through the next two days. Days when he had to concentrate on equations and translations at school, rather than go skipping off to Ash Acre for training sessions. But finally, on Friday evening, thanks to his dad, Luke got an answer. And what an answer it was!

Green Senior didn't get to see much of his dearly-beloved son nowadays. After years as a stupendously unsuccessful singer-guitarist, he had suddenly hit big in the last six months. This was partly a result of him loving football as much as Luke's mum loathed it. Calling himself TAFKAG (The Artist Formerly Known As Green) he had co-written Albion's Cup Final single, "Castle Rap", with Cool F – who had *major* musical talent (and a stage-presence to die for).

TAFKAG meant his dippy hippie warblings to be taken quite seriously. The record-buying public, however, thought they were the funniest thing they'd heard since someone had suggested that Wales might qualify for a World Cup. The single shot to the top of the British chart, Neil Veal signed TAFKAG (featuring Cool F) to his roster, and within days he had secured him a three-album deal.

From there on in, there was no stopping the bloke in the polka-dot bandanna. "Castle Rap" sold in droves from Antigua to Zanzibar. Suddenly his back-catalogue (three deleted singles, a banned EP and eleven albums' worth of previously-unreleased material) became hot property too. Freshly-packaged, it didn't make much impact in Britain but across eastern Europe and into Asia sales were phenomenal. In Bulgaria and Romania TAFKAG was now outselling Madonna. In Uzbekistan he was hailed, slightly puzzlingly, as "the new Celine Dion". While in the Yemen he'd already had an oilfield named after him.

That Friday, he was just back in town after a five-date tour of the western Ukraine. "It went well," he told Luke when he came to fetch him for the weekend. "The language barrier really doesn't appear to be a problem."

Luke smiled to himself at that. "Not a problem." It was an absolute godsend! With lyrics like "*Coconut bath-tubs appear in the sky/ Floating in custard and peas*", it was just as well that hardly anybody overseas understood them.

They travelled in his psychedelically painted van to the five-star hotel where he was staying for the week. He'd driven the rickety old thing all the way to Kiev and back for his latest string of gigs. "She's done me proud over the years," he told Luke. "How could I just chuck her now and start flying? And besides, it's good to be on the road. Keeps me close to my roots, you know?"

"So it's not that you're actually *afraid* of flying?" Luke asked as he picked up a handset in TAFKAG's suite and flicked through all the TV stations on offer.

"Me? *Afraid?*" he laughed through from the jacuzzi. "You're kidding, yeah? No way. Don't get me confused with that Dog guy."

Luke's eyes popped as he hit on some "adult" channels. " 'Dog guy'?" he said.

"You know? The striker Benny signed back in August? The sheep-farmer?"

Luke tore himself away from the TV screen and drifted over to the bathroom doorway. He had to hear more about this. Since cutting "Castle Rap", TAFKAG had been well-in with the club's head honchos. Before Jimbo had baled out cash-strapped Albion, he even used to take some players to away games in his van. Benny, Terry and Ruel still confided in him.

"So who *is* this mystery striker then, Dad?" asked Luke. "The boss keeps dropping hints but that's as far as it goes. You can tell me, can't you?"

"Oh, why not? You'll meet him soon enough. In Munich, let's hope. I've got a copy of the video somewhere. When I get out of here, I'll let you take a snoop."

Video? Luke jumped as a horrible crashing guitar chord rang out. Then another, even nastier than the last. And a third that made up a truly unholy trinity. "Dad," Luke yelled in a panic. "D'you really think it's a good idea to play an electric guitar in the jacuzzi?"

"No, dude," he called back meekly. "You might have a point there."

Thirty minutes later they sat down together to watch The Video. A scuffed-up thing, with foreign writing all over the label. *Seriously* foreign-looking writing. But Luke soon forgot about that as the pictures began to entrance him.

The whole thing lasted only ten minutes. There were clips from about twenty different games, but all in the same ramshackle, almost empty stadium. The players were mostly swarthy and black-haired – a bit like the Turks who had come to Ash Acre with Fenerbahce. But the star from start to finish was a tall, lean striker with powerful legs, a thick black moustache and lots of shaggy hair.

Luke had never seen finishing like it. The guy could score for fun from anywhere in the opposition's half. Left foot, right foot. He even netted one bullet header from fifteen yards *outside* the box. It was frightenlng. OK, so the defences he was up against didn't look exactly red-hot. But he really was different class. That kind of technique just couldn't be bought. Or could it?

"So..." Luke gasped when it was over. "He's ... our new striker?"

"Will be," TAFKAG nodded, removing the video and slotting it back into its cardboard box, on which Luke now noticed a small sticker with the English words:

> **As supplied by Neil Veal,**
> **Agent to the Stars**
> **(Whatever Their Game)**

"Dogan Mezir's his name. Armenian sheep-farmer. Signed up in August. One of Vealy's. He'll be leading our line – once we can get him here."

"But what's holding him up?" asked Luke. "He signed in August, you say?"

"Yeah. Before the season started. He didn't come cheap either! His club really stitched Benny up on that one. Lovely fella though, diamond geezer. It was only afterwards that the – er – snag came to light."

"Snag?"

"Right. He's a bit of a homeboy. Never travelled more than ten miles from his home village. And – well – he won't use any form of powered transport."

"Sorry?"

"Car, bus, train, plane, ship – you name it, he won't travel on it. Panic attacks, blackouts; the whole idea's just too heavy for him. So that's why he's on his way here right now – on a pushbike."

"A bike!"

"All the way from Asia Minor." TAFKAG frowned. "Bad vibe is – he hasn't got much of a sense of direction either. Last time anyone spotted him, he was heading into the mountains of Transylvania. You know, Dracula country? Anyway, I had a chat with Benny last night, and he's had it with waiting around. So he's sending Terry to find him, and get him to Munich in time for the second leg. But hey, with old Dog up front, you'll slaughter those boys from Bayern."

Luke nodded slowly. Now he understood why Jimbo was so opposed to buying Albion into the big time. He'd clearly had his fingers burned with Mr Mezir. Once bitten, twice shy. But, oh, he *did* look tasty.

"Tell you what, Dad," Luke said quickly, as TAFKAG reached out again for his guitar, "let's just take another look at that video, shall we?"

9

TAFKAG had to call in at a local studio on Saturday morning. They needed a few final overdubs for the new album. Next week, Cool F would be adding a couple of his unique raps, then that would be that.

Luke choose not to suffer while his dad did his stuff. It was hard enough listening to him in the jacuzzi. With all that amplification it was an absolute nightmare. So he waited out in the studio foyer, flicking through the newspapers and sport 'n' style magazines on the glass-topped coffee-table.

Luke wasn't the kind of boy to brag, but he counted twenty-four references to himself. In the papers, all the talk was about how he and Cool F deserved full England call-ups despite Albion's pretty awful season so far. In *Total Football* there was a statistical breakdown of his phenomenally accurate passing in the recent clash with Southend. He came out as four times more effective than Tim Sherwood in Spurs' game with Coventry on the same Saturday. Then there were the full-page ads for a variety of products in *GQ, Country Life* and *J17*.

Luke always flinched when he saw one of these. There was no chance of his mum reading the football pages and finding out about him that way but, stuck in a dentist's waiting room, she could easily glance through *Country Life*. And there she'd find him: kitted out for a weekend grouse-shooting expedition, with the words *As worn by all young sharpshooters* under the manufacturer's logo.

He was always photographed from behind, or else from the neck down if shot from the front – and his name was never mentioned. Vealy made dead sure of that. But anyone with half a brain could see who the young sharp-shooter was (or the boy in the butt-hugging jeans, or the laddo catching the bottle of Lucozade). That was the whole point of using him – and paying piles of dosh into his trust fund for the privilege. And surely one day Luke's mum was going to turn a page, look up at a hoarding or catch a TV commercial. And then...

"Hi, Luke," smiled a sound engineer, offering Luke a Coke and a Kit-Kat from the vending machine. "Your dad's in, is he? I wondered what that racket was! I thought you'd be on the road to Cheltenham by now, though."

Luke glanced at his watch. The time *was* getting on a bit. "Reckon you've got any chance today, Luke?" the receptionist called over. "Or will you all be feeling the backlash from your midweek exertions against Bayern?"

Luke grinned back and ripped back the Coke's ring-pull. "We'll give it our best shot," he said. "We can only ever take each game as it comes."

"Take *out* James Prince, more like," put in a producer who was passing through. "You'll never get anywhere with him in the side."

"Doesn't he *know* how bad he is?" asked the receptionist. "Doesn't he read what the papers say about all the games he's thrown away?"

Luke took a slurp of Coke and broke into his Kit-Kat. If he'd been given a pound for every time he'd been asked that question, he could have paid Robbie Fowler's wages for a fortnight. All Luke ever did was shrug and smile, but the answer was no, Jimbo didn't read match reports. Nor did he seem to hear the taunts of all opposition fans. In his mind he was, well – he was Pelé. And if things weren't exactly hunky-dory at Ash Acre, it certainly wasn't *his* fault.

TAFKAG finally emerged and rushed Luke out to his waiting van. "We'll still make it," he assured his son. "Sorry about the hold-up. Eric Clapton did a down-the-line solo on one of the tracks. *Eric!* Once we got rapping about the

Sixties I couldn't stop. Yardbirds, Cream, Blind Faith. Man, that guy's a god!"

No journey in Luke's dad's van was very comfortable. And the way TAFKAG drove to Cheltenham (very quickly, very badly) made Luke gravely carsick by the time they pitched up at the Whaddon Road ground. While TAFKAG parked, he went for a walk on shaky legs to get his bearings again. But as soon as the autograph hunters spotted him, he was swept off his feet altogether. In the end Vealo hurtled out of the players' entrance and pretty well carried his young prodigy inside. Still feeling groggy, Luke smelled burning in the corridor where Veal set him down.

"Hello!" beamed one of two men behind him in white coats (that now had some very sooty stains on them). "Headless Hero!"

"Got to dash," Luke gasped, before he could even get a glimpse of the latest *Lukewarm*, then he made his zig-zaggy way to the away dressing-room.

But as he pushed back the door, the awesome power of the din inside nearly knocked him over. He'd never heard anything like it. Chrissie had sometimes tried to "psych up" the team before games with top-volume Prodigy tapes on his ghetto-blaster. But this! What *was* this?

The rest of the players all looked stunned too.

As Luke shut the door behind him, Craig took such a lame pineapple shot at Carl Davey that the lump of fruit barely grazed the big striker's bottom. Then Luke noticed a flurry of activity over in the corner of the room. That was where the dreadful screeching din was coming from. A huge sound system stood on the floor. And around it – bouncing up and down and fisting the air – danced Jimbo and two minders.

For a full three minutes the performance went on. Everyone else could only gape in wonder. Terry and Ruel had their fingers in their ears, while Benny – eyes tight shut – seemed to be trying to retract his whole head inside his sheepskin coat. Then, blissfully, it was over and silence fell. So did Jimbo – in an exhausted heap of skin, bone and spectacles – on to the nearest bench.

"Whew!" he gasped, waving his fists in a way that looked less pumped-up than clapped-out. " 'Save Your Kisses For Me' – Brotherhood of Man. The 1976 Eurovision Song Contest winner! It doesn't come much better! After an earful of that, how can we possibly *not* be ready to take Cheltenham Town apart!"

"Ri-i-i-ght," said Benny, his head emerging again but his eyes still firmly closed. "As the chairman says: after that, we ought to be able to face anything."

10

As it happened, Albion *weren't* able to face an injury-hit and somewhat off-colour Cheltenham side. Or rather, ten of Benny's players probably *could* have scratched out a result. But one skinny, knock-kneed lad in a baggy number-ten shirt sure couldn't. And that one young party-pooper made all the difference.

But it all started off quite well. In the twelfth minute Luke and Frederick worked a move they had honed to perfection in the park years before. All it took to start it off was a tweak by Frederick on his own left ear. That was the signal.

Cool F then took a roll-out from Madman just outside the penalty box. Without even looking up, he swivelled round and lasered a pass deep into enemy territory along the right flank. Luke, having seen his mate's signal, had already left his marker for dead by racing along the touch-line. By the time he was ten paces short of the ball, he was right behind the entire Cheltenham defence.

Rocky Mitford and the travelling 764 un-leashed a tumult that sounded as if it came from the throats of ten thousand. Meanwhile, with half the Robins' side frantically back-pedalling, Cool F had set off on a lightning-fast run though the middle. He seemed to be gliding over the turf, not touching it at all as he honed in ever-closer to the opposition's goal.

Suddenly everyone in the stadium saw what was about to happen. The cheek of these kids! They were going to play a pitch-length one-two! Frederick to Luke then back to Frederick, who would surely then hammer in a first-time shot – bypassing the whole Cheltenham outfield and beating the hapless keeper!

The guy in dark green didn't know *what* to do. He'd left it too late to hurtle out and hoof the ball into the stand before Luke reached it. Now he was in two minds whether to narrow Luke's angle or stay put and try to intercept the cross that he was about to swing over to the oncom-ing Frederick. Rocky and Co's roar rose even louder. Luke caught up with the ball just as it obligingly stopped rolling and sat up waiting to be pinged in.

One glance was all he needed. The keeper might have been in two minds. Luke wasn't. He swung his trusty right leg back, but instead of scooping the ball across the face of the goal with his instep, he struck it quite beautifully with the *outside* of his trainer. Up it soared into the air – not towards Cool F, who had already stopped his run to admire his mate's awesome accuracy, but way over the stranded keeper's head. Then down it dipped when it was past him, sinking slowly under the crossbar and low into the corner of the net. Nil-one!

Seven hundred and sixty-five travelling Albion supporters went spare. Up leapt Benny, Terry, Ruel and the subs with a yell of their own that almost matched it. Then Luke wheeled away to be smothered by ten screaming team-mates. He'd done it again. His ninth strike of the season. Albion were ahead!

But this, unfortunately, was as good as it got for CAFC on that particular overcast afternoon. From here on in, only one team beginning with C was going to win. And from this point on, only a player with the initials JP mattered.

As usual, Benny had ordered his chairman to stay upfield at all times. But after he was caught offside for the sixteenth time, even Benny started waving him back a bit. Almost inevitably then, as the half-hour struck, Jimbo was caught in possession forty-five yards out from Albion's goal. As his dispossessor raced away towards Madman, JP decided to give chase.

"No, no!" shouted everyone from Madman to Luke. "Stay upfield, James! *Don't come back!*" But – still fired up from "Save Your

Kisses For Me" – Jimbo wouldn't listen. Clumsily he snapped at the number four's heels for fifteen yards until he brought him clattering down and conceded the free kick. He got a yellow card for his trouble. Cheltenham scored direct from the kick. And twenty-two minutes into the second half, in a carbon copy of the move that had brought the home team's equalizer, Jimbo hacked down the number four again.

Luke gasped in anticipation as the ref whistled. Another free kick, definitely. Possibly Albion would concede another goal. But wasn't this JP's second bookable offence? He would have to get his marching orders! An early bath!

No such luck. Cheltenham got the kick, then from it they got their second goal. But the ref took a lenient view of the player-chairman's challenge and let him off with a verbal roasting. Apart from JP himself, Luke and Frederick were the only Albion players who didn't close in furiously on the referee. They were pretending to dispute the free kick. But in reality every one of them was urging the ref to rethink his decision and send their own number ten off the field.

It did no good. James Prince lasted the full ninety minutes. And, despite a late blaster from Cool F that almost cracked the Cheltenham crossbar, there was no way back for Albion.

They trudged from the field with their shoulders drooping and with jeers ringing in their ears from all the home fans. There were even some catcalls from the Albion ranks.

Now this was unusual. Dirt-poor though Jimbo was as a player, the Albion fans knew they owed him a huge debt for saving their club from extinction. For months they had made the best of a bad job with him. But now even *their* patience was beginning to wear thin. "It's time to abdicate, Prince!" Luke heard someone holler from the Albion seats. Glancing up, he saw it was a TV sitcom star who'd just declared a lifelong, previously hidden, passion for the Albion.

"*I'm* better than you are, Mr Jimbo!" screamed another voice close by, this time a young woman's. Luke had heard her chanting for Chrissie every time he got near the touchline. Now he saw her: a staggeringly smart new supermodel. (What did they all *see* in him? he wondered – great bloke though Chrissie undoubtedly was.)

"Forget about it, lads," said a grey-faced Benny back in the dressing room. "Lincoln at home next Wednesday. Let's all focus on that one now."

But later, at the post-match press conference, he finally cracked. The moment came when, for the umpteenth time that season, he was asked:

"Where are the goals going to come from, Benny? With the team as it is now, you're never going to keep a clean sheet, so you've got to score more goals than the opposition. But apart from Luke Green and Frederick Dulac, who aren't even strikers, no one's hitting the net for you. *Why don't you buy a striker?*"

"I have bought a striker!" Benny moaned back, lifting his great troubled head from his hands. "I *have* bought one, believe me. Oh, all right, I'll tell you..."

Then, at last, as microphones bristled, tape-recorders whirred and pencils raced across the pages of journalists' notepads, Benny Webb broke the news to the waiting world about an Armenian goal-machine by the name of Dogan Mezir.

11

WHAT A MEZ! said just about every sports-page headline – not just in Sunday's newspapers, but in Monday's as well.

ROVING STRIKER'S LONG ROAD TO ALBION laughed The *Guardian*.

MUCH-TRAVELLED MARKSMAN AIMS FOR UEFA GLORY ... EVENTUALLY! chortled The *Daily Mail*.

HE HASN'T GOT A DOG'S CHANCE OF MAKING IT TO MUNICH! giggled The *Mirror*.

It was just as well that Benny hadn't told them the whole story. All he'd said was that a sleek new superstriker *had* been signed, but that currently he was having problems with his "travel arrangements". So, to help him out, Terry V had been sent to ensure that he arrived in time for the second-leg game with Bayern. And then – Benny the Beard confidently predicted – with Deadly Dogan in place, no defence in Europe would be able to contain them.

"But who's going to get dropped so he can

play?" Carl Davey asked, a little nervously, before they all went out for training on Monday morning.

The boss stared back. He knew how to use this situation. "The way you lot played on Saturday," he said, "it could be any one from eight. Luke and Frederick will always be the first names on any teamsheet of mine. As for the rest of you – it's still up to you to convince me that you're *worth* your places."

There was an outbreak of muttering and grumbling. Not many of the squad had top grades in GCSE Maths. Luke could almost *see* Madman, Chrissie, Narris and the rest trying to work out the sum in their heads: "any one from eight", Benny had said. Plus Luke and Frederick. That made ten. Who, then, was the other dead cert for the ultra-glamorous Bayern fixture?

"Oh no, Boss!" Half-Fat suddenly exclaimed, after looking left and right to check that the player-chairman was, once again, absent from training. "You *can't* keep Jimbo in the side after Cheltenham! It's unreal!"

"He's shot us in the foot so many times," Dennis agreed, "there's hardly any foot left for him to aim at!"

"Ooh, that's a nice turn of phrase," cooed Craig, his novel-writing partner, reaching for his pen. "We'll use that."

Before anyone else could protest Benny raised both arms in the air. "Lads, lads!" he boomed, looking up. "You know as well as I do that my hands are tied on this one." Then, a bit sheepishly, he let his arms fall and put his hands behind his back. "Much as I might *like* to have a freer hand in team-selection matters, the chairman's got me over a barrel. If *he* don't play, *we* don't play. It's as simple as that. He could pull the plug on this club just as quick as he – er – put the plug in, in the first place. *None of us can afford to upset him*. And I don't have to tell you: he's already *well* upset at the way this season's gone."

Luke saw the haunted look in the boss's eyes. For weeks Big Ben hadn't been his old self. The pressure from JP was really getting to him. Already three papers were saying that he would get the chop if Albion went down in Munich. And unless someone had a bright idea pretty soon, Luke himself wouldn't be making the trip to Germany to play in the game that would decide Benny's fate.

"We can still crock Jimbo, though, can't we?" asked Madman brightly.

"*How*, Piebrain?" roared Gaffer, clipping the keeper round the ear. "He's never here for training! None of us can get near him!"

"Yes – um – Mr Prince had to leave first thing this morning for an emergency meeting in

Capetown," Benny explained. "He sends his apologies."

"Apologies most definitely not accepted!" Narris spat back. "Unless of course he's not going to be able to get back in time for the Lincoln game."

"Well, that *is* the pot of gold at the end of this little rainbow," Benny went on. "There's no way he'll be back for Wednesday night. And the chances are that he won't make it for Swansea away on Saturday either..."

The triumphant chorus which met *that* piece of news would have drowned out eight Eurovision winners from Jimbo's ghetto-blaster.

"So this is our chance, lads," Ruel took over from Benny when the din died down. "We can put a few League points in the bank this week, then go to Germany without having to look back over our shoulders. Now get out there on to that pitch and let's train like it's going out of fashion!"

"I wish it *would* go out of fashion," Dennis said to Carl as they all jostled their way out into the corridor. "I'm miles behind on my bit of the novel. I could do with a few free mornings just to catch up."

"You concentrate on pounding around that bit of grass, Dennis lad," said Benny. He had elephant ears. "*Then* you can pound away on your typewriter."

Luke, the last out, felt the boss's hand on his shoulder. "Luke, son, where's Frederick got to this mornin'? I thought he'd be arriving with you."

"No, Boss," Luke told him. "He wasn't at school. They must have had a late session at the studio last night. He was overdubbing some raps for my dad's new album. He'll probably come straight on when they've finished."

Benny shook his head sadly. "Writing novels. Overdubbing raps. Modelling men's clothes. Alf Ramsey never had players bunking off for reasons like that when he guided England to World Cup victory in 1966! I tell you, son, sometimes I wonder what football's comin' to. It certainly wasn't all the extra-terrestrial activity that made *me* fall in love with the game, way back when."

Luke looked up at him puzzled, but then a voice from the doorway piped up: "Er, I think you'll find that's 'extra-*curricular*', Mr Webb," said the man holding the boom-mike for the fly-on-the-wall team. They had been filming all this from out in the corridor. "Extra-curricular: stuff that people do outside their normal daily jobs. Extra-*terrestrial* means aliens." He paused with a thin smile. "Would you like to do that last bit again?"

Benny glared at him, every hair in his beard seeming to bristle. "I'll do *you*, my son, if you're not careful. Get a life, can't you? All of you! You should be ashamed of yourselves – you're just a bunch of Peepin' Toms!"

He patted Luke on the back, sending him out to join the rest of the squad. "And you know the score on that young lad too," he fumed at the TV team as he followed Luke out. "If you've filmed an *inch* above his neck, you can forget about showing even a minute of this drivel on the telly!"

12

"Luke!" screamed his mum from the foot of the stairs at nine thirty on Tuesday evening. "Get down here this minute!"

Luke got up from his desk like someone summoned to the electric chair. He feared the worst. The absolute worst. Ten minutes earlier he had heard the phone ring. His toes had curled at once in his trainers. Cutlet? Mr Mallard? (That was Rodney's code-name for Benny – Webb = webbed feet = duck = mallard.) They didn't ring often, but when they did it was usually on the eve of a game. Yet no one had called him down from his room ... until now.

His mum was waiting in the lounge with folded arms. The look on her face was puzzled rather than furious. Rodney was blinking behind her, hopping from foot to foot like a baby sparrow that hadn't yet worked out how to take off.

"I've just had your headmistress on the phone," Luke's mum began.

"Yes?" He racked his brain for anything bad that he'd done at school recently.

"What's up, Luke?" she asked. "You look terribly guilty. Is there something you'd like to tell me about?"

Behind her, Rodney hopped and blinked more manically than ever. But now he was shaking his head at Luke too and mouthing: No, *No!*

"Er ... no," Luke replied, blushing. "But what did the head want?"

"Well, it's all rather peculiar. And *very* sudden. It seems that the school has fixed up a number of exchanges with children from schools in Germany. Pupils in your year are going to go and stay with families there. Then the children from *those* families will come and spend some time here..."

"Enormous educational benefits to be had," Rodney put in, nodding now. "Wish I'd had a chance like this when *I* was at school."

"Ah now, I'm not so sure," Luke's mum said, her brow furrowing more deeply. "It seems like an awful lot of upheaval to me – just so that Luke can have a couple of days in ... where was it? Bavaria?"

"Bavaria, yes," nodded Rodney, flashing a meaningful look at Luke. "What the Germans call *Bayern*, I believe. And Luke would be going to stay with a family that lives right in the centre of Munich! Oh, what an opportunity for him!"

It had taken a while, but now a light went on in Luke's brain. So *this* was how Benny and the head were hoping to get him to the UEFA Cup away leg.

"What do *you* think, Luke?" his mum asked – her scowl making it pretty clear what answer she wanted to hear from him.

He blew out his cheeks. Behind his mum, Rodney was now hopping, blinking, nodding, giving Luke the thumbs-up with both hands *and* mouthing, Yesss!

"Well, as Rodney says, it *would* be a brilliant opportunity for me. Er – when would I be going, exactly?"

"This is the ridiculous thing. Next week! It's all such a mad rush. I mean, we'd hardly have time to buy you all the things you'd need to take."

"Oh, I shouldn't think we'd have to *buy* him anything, dear," Rodney blurted.

She turned on him fiercely, just catching the end of his hop, blink and thumbs-up routine. "He would be representing us in a foreign country, Rodney," she declared. "He would have to look his best. Have you seen the state of his socks and underpants recently? And those dreadful mud-encrusted trainers he always wears – those things his father bought without even consulting me? Honestly, if I didn't know better, I'd think he was playing *football* in them!"

"Oh no, dear. Not that. Never that!" gasped Rodney, trying to look aghast. Luke too began to shake his head, hard, when she looked back at him.

"So – as I say," she continued, "we would have to undertake a major shopping expedition if you were to think of making this trip. And I just don't know if I can fit that in at such short notice. I'm a very busy woman. Then, on top of that, I'd have to start thinking about having a German girl *here* later on..."

"Girl?" spluttered Luke.

"Why, yes. The person the school has linked you up with is a young woman of exactly your age. Ursula. The head knows her family personally. But if you went there, she would have to come here in return. That's what exchanges are all about. And the spare room is in *such* a mess at the moment..."

"Don't you worry yourself about that, dear," said Rodney, rubbing his hands and becoming quite masterful. "I'll get the room shipshape. And I'll take this young lad shopping too – if you can't fit it into your own busy schedule. I really do think we should try to move heaven and earth if it means we'll be able to get Luke on to that pitch..." He gulped, realizing – too late – his horrible mistake.

"*Pitch?*" repeated Luke's mum, raising one eyebrow so high that it threatened to disappear right up into her hair.

"Yes, er, pitch," Rodney burbled, his face as red as a Southampton stripe. "Pitch. It's, ah, a German word, my dear. *Pitch.*" He said it again, pronouncing it like "peach" this time. "*Der Pitch.* And it means... Oh, what does it mean? *Yes!* It means ... an aeroplane! Old Luftwaffe slang. From the way planes *pitch* and roll during turbulence. That's what it means, doesn't it, Luke? *Der Pitch* – an aeroplane!"

Luke's mum didn't even bother to turn and watch her son nodding dumbly. She smelled a rat here. You could almost hear her nostrils quivering.

"The more I think about this whole escapade," she said finally, "the less I like the sound of it... Now, if neither of you has any objection, I intend to spend the next hour soaking in the bath." And with that she stalked out.

"Don't say a thing!" Rodney hissed at Luke as soon as she was out of earshot. "I'll make up for my mistake. I promise I will. I'll keep on at her about this trip until she lets you go just to shut me up." Then he winced. "Oh I'm such a *fool*!"

13

After school on Wednesday Luke went straight to his dad's hotel suite where he was going to sleep over. It was TAFKAG's last night in town before setting off on a ten-date tour of Uruguay. Luckily, that coincided with Albion's home game against Lincoln. So Luke thought he'd have none of his usual mum-made problems over getting to the match. But still she managed to put her oar in.

Just as father and son were leaving, the phone rang. TAFKAG snatched up the receiver, and from the way he said "Oh hi!" Luke could tell it was his mum. "As it happens," he went on, after a pause, "we're just on our way out..."

Another, longer, pause followed. "Oh yeah?" he asked, making a face at Luke. "You can see idiotic people streaming past on their way to the *football* ground...?" (Luke's house on Cranham Hill was just a stone's throw away from Ash Acre.) "What? No way! ... No *way* am I taking Luke to see any football match tonight... Look, you can stay completely cool on this one..." He put his free hand on his quilted paisley waistcoat. "With my hand on my heart, I swear to you on the Beatles' White Double-Album that Luke will be watching no football match tonight! OK now? Catch you later!"

"D'you think she believed you?" asked Luke as they left the room.

"Why shouldn't she?" said TAFKAG, a bit shakily. "I told her no lie. I mean, you won't be *watching* tonight, will you? Playing, yes. Watching, no way."

The hotel was near the outskirts of town, but when TAFKAG drove Luke off in his van he appeared to be heading even further out. "Shouldn't we – er – be going *into* town?" Luke asked. Sometimes his dad could be a bit scatty.

"All in good time," the old boy grinned back, adjusting his multi-coloured headband. "First off though, we've got to see a man about a shoe."

"A shoe? Oh no – not the *Lukewarm* again!"

"Vealy thought it might be best to give this model an open-air trial," TAFKAG explained, peering out into the early evening darkness. "It tends to get a bit smoky in enclosed spaces. So he suggested a quick five-minute session outside the new Majestic Stadium." He grabbed Luke's knee and shook it fondly.

Luke rolled his eyes. "New Majestic

Stadium" was pushing it. As they veered off the road down a rough bumpy track, all he could see ahead was a massive building site, with a great heap of scaffolding poking up in the middle. One day a spanking new stadium complex *might* stand there. But not for some time yet.

TAFKAG pulled up abruptly, making Luke feel sicker than ever. "This place will really be the business!" he purred, staring misty-eyed at the scaffolding. "Jimbo's already booked me to play a couple of tunes at the opening ceremony. Wow – I'm getting the vibes already. Bit different from old Ash Acre, eh?"

Luke gazed out, unconvinced. As it happened, with all that rubble around, it *didn't* look very much different from Ash Acre. Not at the moment. He pictured how it would look when it was finished. He'd seen plenty of artists' drawings of the stadium itself. Like a great spiky bathtub for 25,000 spectators, it would be. Stuck in the middle of nowhere. No, not nowhere. In the middle of a gigantic car-park.

Luke knew he was meant to be excited about this new chapter in the history of his beloved club (founded 1872). But he couldn't help thinking he would miss Ash Acre – nestling in amongst all those narrow lamplit streets. It was falling apart and it had grass all over the terraces and black redstarts nesting in the main stand and the tannoy never worked and the burgers were less edible than the soles of a pair of *Lukewarms*, but it was home. And Luke still loved it.

"There we go," cried TAFKAG, nodding to his right and struggling to open the van door. "There's Vealy and the boffins!"

Luke peered harder through the windscreen. He could just make out three figures – one wearing a Boss suit and Rayban shades (on a December night!), the other two in their white coats. But they all seemed to be running. Towards the van. *Away* from what Luke had thought was a workman's burning brazier.

"Back!" Veal was yelling in a strangled voice as his tie flew over his shoulder. "Get the van back! She's gonna blow!"

Then all three flung themselves headlong on to the churned-up ground – and the "brazier" exploded in a fizz of brilliant orange sparks and flames.

"Holy Rolling Stones!" murmured TAFKAG, tearing off the handbrake and backing up the van. "I think that must have been the *Lukewarm Mark Four*."

Luke could only gulp. It most certainly had been. If he'd tried the thing on just seconds before, he wouldn't just be Headless now but Legless as well. But the dodgy trainer soon burned itself out. And a mud-spattered Vealo was back on his feet, grinning and mouthing "Have a good one!" at Luke as TAFKAG ferried him away again towards his date with the Imps of Lincoln City.

14

There was a different buzz in the Albion dressing-room when Luke arrived. No prizes for guessing why: Jimbo wasn't inside it!

"This is more like it, eh lads?" roared Carl after taking a stinging pineapple-hit from Craig. "No one to mess it all up on the pitch!"

"Oh, I dunno about that," muttered Benny. "Not with some of you lot."

Which was a fair comment. You never knew quite what you were going to get with this bunch of players. They had, after all, finished twenty-third out of twenty-four in Division Three last season, as well as winning the FA Cup.

"But at least there's no one to make us sit through any more Eurovision Song Contest winners!" Half-Fat chirped.

"Ah," Ruel cut in, looking horribly embarrassed. "Now that you mention it, Jimbo *did* leave behind a little something for you all." To a wave of groans from everyone in the room, he produced the club ghetto-blaster from behind his back, set it down on the physio's bench and switched it on. "He picked out 'Puppet on a String' by Sandie Shaw – the 1967 winner, apparently. Said he knew you'd get a real kick out of hearing it." He stared down glumly at the machine.

Everybody braced themselves, eyes shut, faces twisted up in pain – and that was even before any noise flooded out of the speakers. Two more seconds passed. Three. Five. Still the room stayed silent except for the machine's hum.

"Hold up, Ruel," said Gaffer, taking a finger out of one ear. "What's going on?"

Ruel continued to gaze down at the whirring machine. It was definitely on. The hand-picked cassette inside was definitely going round. "The chairman made me promise to play this tape at precisely this time," he explained. "But he didn't say a word about how *loudly* I should play it."

Slowly a smile spread across his face. Amid hoots of relieved laughter all round, Luke took a closer peek at the ghetto-blaster to find the volume dial fixed firmly on zero.

"Right, cheers Ruel," said Benny when the silent tape finally clicked off and everyone jumped up ready for action. "I reckon that's done us all a power of good. Now get out there under those floodlights, in this theatre of footballing dreams, and do the same thing to Lincoln as Mr John Wilkes Booth did!"

That brought puzzled looks from just about everyone. "Come again, Boss?" asked Narris. "What's that you said?" enquired Chrissie. "Who does John Wilkes Booth play for then? Is it Forest?" queried Dennis. "Nah," said Craig, "That's Chris Bart-Williams."

Benny's losing it, Luke thought with a stab of panic. All this pressure – it's really starting to affect his brain.

The boss closed his eyes. "Stone me, you lot! Don't you know *nothin'*?" A dozen pairs of eyes looked back blankly. "Lincoln, right? *Abraham* Lincoln? Big American President? Beard? Freed the slaves?" One or two players murmured yes, but not very confidently. Then Cool F nodded.

"Respect, Boss," he grinned. "JWB was the dude who shot Lincoln dead at the theatre. Now you want *us* to go out and gun down Lincoln *City* – right?"

"R-i-g-h-t!" Benny sighed. "Sometimes I wonder why I bother. Off you all go."

They charged out into the tunnel, and Luke could see how confused some of the players still looked. But as soon as the game got under way, no one in an Albion shirt gave another thought to Benny's bewildering pep-talk. And no one put himself about more than the lad from the soccer academy wearing Jimbo's number ten shirt for the night. This was Keats Aberdeen – named after the famous English poet by his book-loving mum (but always called "Keith" by Benny).

Keats wasn't much bigger than Princey. But he had a whole lot more going for him as a footballer. Ruel had high hopes for him once he'd filled out.

"He's Po-etry in Motion!"

Rocky and the Southsiders blasted out after a mazy run in the seventeenth minute that left four Lincoln defenders trailing.

Luke had forgotten what it was like to aim through-balls at a number ten who didn't immediately fall over, run the wrong way, or get blown up for offside. Carl too struck up a great understanding with the rookie. They worked one-two's with each other as if they'd been playing in harness all season. Every time Carl flicked it on, there was Keatsy running on to it. And every time the Ambitious Aberdeen back-heeled it, there was Carl to pick it up.

Benny was entranced. "It's like they're tele-pathetic," Luke heard him saying to Ruel when Keatsy went over to take a throw. "That's tele*pathic*, Mr Webb," Luke then heard the fly-on-the-wall man correcting him. "Shall we go again?"

But for all Albion's pressure, the score stayed at nil-nil till well into the second half. Lincoln were no soft touch – as their seventh place in the table showed – and they got plenty of bodies back to keep their goal intact. The longer the game went on, the fewer clear-cut chances Albion made. Part of the problem now was Keatsy. After seventy-two minutes he'd run himself into the ground and all he could fire was blank verse.

To a huge round of applause Benny called him off and sent on another promising young academy graduate, lanky Casper Franks, in his place. Within minutes the game finally tilted Albion's way. Casper wasn't as speedy as Keats, but with the ball at his feet he just seemed to ghost his way towards goal, leaving the Lincoln defenders flailing at thin air. Until, that was, with seventy-five minutes gone, one of them made contact and hacked him to the deck. And since the Albion sub was four yards inside the Lincoln box at the time, the ref had no hesitation whatever in whistling for a pen.

Up stepped Luke. Now, if you needed someone to take a spot-kick to save your life, Luke Green was your boy. Sometimes he blasted it, sometimes he stroked it. Sometimes he went right, sometimes he went straight down the middle. With Luke, it all just depended on how the fancy took him.

As the Albion faithful hushed up now – and the 469 from Lincoln at the far end made the most hideous racket to try to put him off – he noticed the Imps' keeper leaning quite sharply to his left. So Luke glanced to the netminder's right. The keeper saw and began to sway that way. But just as Luke made to shoot, he looked way over to the keeper's *left* again. The poor guy in gloves seemed to seize up. Not knowing which way to dive, his legs stayed rooted to the line. Then, before he knew it, Luke sidefooted the ball between them into the goal!

Ash Acre erupted. The tannoy gave out after "The scorer of tonight's first..." but Rocky and Co were yelling too loud for any announcement to be heard. They kept on chanting all the way through to the final whistle.

"We're Going Up To Fifteenth!
We're Going Up To Fifteenth!"

they chorused joyfully when the ref signalled full-time. And indeed Albion were. It had been a close-run thing, but they'd nabbed three much-needed League points. Heading off the pitch, Luke had his back slapped so many times that his spine began to sting.

"I don't care *who* that John Wilkes Booth plays for, or *what* he did to Lincoln," roared Craig after an especially hard whack between Luke's shoulder-blades, "But I bet he's *never* put a pen through a goalkeeper's legs!"

15

Two nights later Luke had a weird dream. He was in a jampacked football ground. It must have been Bayern's Olympiastadion, because he was lining up to take a penalty against Oliver Kahn, Munich's German-international keeper.

The crowd noise was incredible. But there was also another sound, closer by. A kind of humming, like a motor. Or two motors. Glancing down, Luke saw that he was wearing the *Lukewarms*, both of them streaming smoke.

Suddenly his feet got terribly hot. He began to hop up and down, desperate to put out the fires that were burning under his soles. As the smoke grew thicker, his team-mates gathered round and tried to put him out. But they seemed to be ignoring his feet, and all they did was clap him on the back. Hard, harder, harder still. Then someone grabbed hold of his hand. *Really* hard.

Whoever this was, he appeared to want to crush every bone in Luke's right hand. "No!"

Luke choked through the smoke. "No, let go! It's my *feet*!"

"Yes, I know it's your feet, young man," said a rich, familiar voice close to his ear. "It's your nifty little feet that are going to take Castle Albion all the way through to Rome!"

What *was* this? The voice of God? Slowly all the smoke faded. The stadium dissolved. Luke fought to open his eyes and wake right up from the dream. But he still felt enormous pressure on his hand. He could almost *hear* the bones being scrunched together down there. "Rome, my lad!" the voice was still whispering. "The UEFA Cup Final! And you'll take Albion there – I know it."

Luke felt his hand being shaken now, his arm being pumped along with it. At last he was able to jerk his eyes open – to find that in the grey light of dawn, a white-haired old man really was talking and shaking his hand. Not God though. It was Luke's football-mad grandpa.

"Aha!" he cried at his favourite grandson. "Welcome to the land of the living!"

Luke grinned blearily and tried to return the vice-like pressure. That was a lost cause. His mum's dad could crumple up a human skull with one of those hands.

"Your nan and I have just popped in on our way to the airport," the old fellow announced in his broad Yorkshire accent. "Surprise visit!"

Then he glanced over his shoulder and said in the softer voice he'd used before, "And we wanted to wish you all the best for Wednesday night too." Again he checked to see if anyone who loathed football was hovering nearby. "Old Rodney's working on your mum round the clock. I'm sure she'll let you travel in the end. And listen – your nan and I will be there too! We've got tickets!"

"Wednesday night?" whispered Luke, managing to tug his hand free and rubbing it to get the circulation going again. "In Munich? For the game?"

"Ssssshhh!" he said, putting a finger to his lips. "The walls have ears here, my lad. Yes, your Mr Veal sent us a couple of complimentaries. Air tickets too."

Luke frowned at that. The Man in Raybans hadn't mentioned that to *him*. But before he could ask his grandpa what airline Vealy had fixed them up with, his mum yelled that breakfast was ready.

Luke gave his nan a big hug in the kitchen. She'd brought croissants and Danish pastries and cereal and yoghurts for everyone to eat. She knew from experience that her daughter's breakfast menu featured only toast (burnt) or toast (badly burnt). Luke and Rodney fell ravenously on the food, while Nan squeezed fresh oranges and brewed up some gorgeous-smelling filter coffee.

"I wish you'd *said* you were calling in," Luke's mum scowled from the doorway. "I could have laid on a proper breakfast."

Nan stifled a smile at that. "Oh don't you worry, dear," she said. "We didn't know we were coming ourselves until yesterday. It's a spur-of-the-moment thing. Hamburg first. Then Munich. It all stemmed from you telling us about Luke's chance to go to Germany. We thought: *we* haven't been to Germany for ages. And we do so like going to the big operas there – don't we, dear?"

"Oh aye," beamed Grandpa, tipping Luke a wink. "Huge Wagner fans, us two. Fantastic atmosphere. We love being in among all that wonderful singing. It's as much as we can do, sometimes, to stop ourselves from joining in!"

Opera indeed, thought Luke. The old couple liked music well enough, but they *loved* football – even if they weren't allowed to mention it in the presence of their daughter. It was good to know they'd be there in the Olympiastadion on Wednesday night. Luke always played even better in front of his grandparents.

But still he wondered exactly what sort of a deal Veal had struck for them. And after breakfast they had to rush off so fast that he didn't get a chance to quiz them further.

Maybe, though, he was just being unfair to

his agent. There was probably nothing in any way dodgy about what he'd fixed up. Nothing whatsoever.

16

That Saturday was an odd day all round for Luke. It started oddly with his grandparents' flying visit. Then, slowly but surely, it got odder still.

He'd known for days that he wouldn't be able to make the game at Swansea. TAFKAG was off on his travels again. Rodney had to go into the office. The head couldn't really invent another school event so soon after fixing up the "German exchange". Luke had simply run out of alibis. (And he could hardly say he was going for a bike ride as cover for getting to Wales and back.)

But even if he'd *had* a cast-iron reason for being out of the house for nine hours, it wouldn't have done him any good. Not as far as his mum was concerned. Because she had made a decision. A big one. Setting aside all her own pressing commitments that afternoon (a visit to the garden centre followed by tea with Auntie Evelyn), she announced that she would, after all, be taking Luke on a shopping expedition prior to his trip to Germany.

"Does that—?" Rodney gasped from the sink where he was washing up. "Does that mean you're actually going to let Luke *go*?"

"Well, I won't be buying him a whole new wardrobe just for fun!" she snapped.

"Oh, that's marvellous, my dear!" Rodney gushed as Luke felt his own heart swell. "It'll be *such* a great experience for the boy. He'll never forget it!"

She narrowed her eyes at Luke. "No, maybe not. But I'll expect him to be fluent in German when he gets back. This trip isn't about having a good time."

"Right, mum," said Luke, nodding solemnly. "I promise not to enjoy myself." But under the table he crossed his fingers on both hands – and his ankles.

After lunch the two of them drove to town and hit the shops. That wasn't quite as straightforward as it might sound. Wherever Luke went nowadays, people of all ages were prone to shout things at him like "Nice pen against Lincoln, Luke!" "Gonna stuff those Germans, then?" or "Do you think your European commitments are distracting you from that all-important push for promotion to Division Two?" Sometimes gangs of kids besieged him for autographs too.

So, just to be on the safe side while he was with his mum, Luke did his best to disguise himself. He couldn't exactly use the cowboy hat, false beard and shades that he'd used to get into Ash Acre with Cool F. That would *really* have made his mum suspicious. But he made do with an old balaclava helmet, plus a scarf wrapped round his face from the eyes down *and* one of Rodney's naffest old puffer jackets, which covered pretty well all the rest of him. "I think I might have a cold coming on," he mumbled to his mum from inside the scarf and pretended to shudder. "I'm feeling a bit chilly."

It took her *hours* to get everything she wanted. If they went into one shop, they must have gone into thirty – every one of them blasting out so much heat that Luke thought he was melting inside all his layers. She'd made a list, which she kept on looking at, but wouldn't let Luke see. In fact, he wasn't sure why she needed him with her at all.

She never made him try on any of the shirts, trousers, pullovers or coats – just held them up against him, muttering to herself. She could just as easily have brought a life-size cardboard cut-out of her son and let *him* shoot off to Swansea. And from what Luke gathered on their travels, he really should have been down there on the south Welsh coast, flying the flag for the Albion.

In several of the smaller shops they were playing the local radio station – which was relaying live commentary from the Vetch Field, Swansea. Each time Luke's mum heard the excitable commentator's voice, she turned right round and left the shop. (That was one reason why the whole expedition took so long.) But Luke dragged his heels and just about managed to piece together the fiasco that was unfolding in the Land of Song.

The first disaster was that Luke's place hadn't been taken by Casper Franks, as he had imagined it would. Instead, Keats Aberdeen had been pulled back into midfield to make space for someone else up front. Someone who hadn't been expected to make the game, but had flown in from New York just minutes before the kick-off. Jetlagged Jimbo! The Prince was back on his throne!

The second disaster was that Narris got sent off in the sixty-third minute. For foul and abusive language. At a member of his own team. Jimbo again – after he'd handled the ball on the edge of the Albion area. *Off* went Narris. *In* went what turned out to be Swansea's free-kick winner. *Bananas* went Benny, no doubt.

Disaster number three occurred in all the remaining twenty-seven minutes. Because in all that time, Jimbo himself did not get crocked. (In spite of what the commentator called "nasty accidental collisions" with Gaffer, Half-Fat and Carl.) So Albion hadn't just lost another three points. Princey would now be playing in Munich.

Luke's shoulders were sagging inside the puffer jacket as his mum led him into their last shop of the afternoon. He was so sick about Swansea that he hardly noticed where they were: a musty old-fashioned shoe-shop. "Yes, ma'am," said an oily assistant in a three-piece suit. "How may I be of service?"

"I want shoes for him," she replied, pointing at Luke. "*Shoes*. Not trainers. Black. Leather. No logos. No *hint* of sport about them. Is that clear?"

"Clear as a bell, ma'am," grinned the creepy suit. "We'll sort Sonny-Jim out."

Thirty minutes later Luke owned the most grotesque pair of shoes he had ever seen. Out of fashion? Out of this world, more like. Even in the Saddo Seventies, kids wouldn't have been seen dead in these. He'd protested that they didn't fit – like the other twelve pairs he had been forced to try on. But it did no good. "All Sonny-Jim needs to do is break them *in*," the weary assistant leered into his face, looking ready to break his toes too if that would make them fit.

"They'll do nicely," announced Luke's mum. "He'll start wearing them now."

While she breezed off to pay, Luke stood clutching his treasured trainers. At least, he thought, he could still pack *these* and wear them all through his stay in Germany. But, oh no. When his mum came back she plucked them from his hands with a look of deep disgust and dropped them into the assistant's arms.

"Would you mind disposing of these?" she said before marching out. "Sonny-Jim won't be having any further use for them. Come on now, Luke. Keep up!"

17

Rodney drove Luke to Heathrow straight after school on Monday. His stepson was still in shock from Saturday afternoon in the shoe-shop.

Rodney knew all about that – and to be fair to him, he looked just as shattered. He knew how much those old trainers meant to Luke. "Well, I've let Benny know what's happened," he said, shaking his head sorrowfully as they entered the terminal. "He's said he'll get you a new pair in Munich."

"But that's not the point," Luke sighed. "Those trainers were special. I played my first game for Albion in them. I wore them at *Wembley*."

Rodney blinked and chewed his lip. "Oh Luke, I know how you must feel. Sick as a parrot, right? It would be like me losing my birdwatching binoculars – the ones I've had for twenty years."

"But I didn't *lose* my trainers," Luke couldn't help pointing out. "I know exactly where they are. Or were. I went there at lunchtime today to try and get them back."

Rodney turned to Luke and blinked hard. "You went to the shoe shop? What happened?"

"That prat of a bloke who works there told me to get lost. He said he'd thrown them away on Saturday night."

A glint came into Rodney's eyes behind his glasses. "Maybe..." he murmured. "Just maybe..."

"What?" asked Luke.

Rodney gripped his arm and squeezed it, teeth clenched, jaw quivering – he looked as if he was about to fight a duel. "I'm not promising you anything, Luke. So don't get your hopes up. But I'll see what I can do about this. I'll give it my best shot for you, I swear." He nodded. "Oh look, there they all are."

The rest of the squad – minus Jimbo, who was jetting out in his own plane on Wednesday – had already checked in. After some turmoil before the flights to Malta and Turkey, Benny had insisted that everyone arrive a full four hours before take-off. Today that gave him time to send Chrissie home for the passport he'd forgotten. Then he made sure Craig took his travel-sickness pills, frisked Madman (who didn't trust foreign food) for meat pies, Scotch eggs and fish fingers – and removed the pine-apple Carl Davey had hidden in his luggage.

"I've told you over and over!" the boss ranted. "Germany's knee-deep in pineapples. We'll get you one there. And yes, Luke – we'll get you some new trainers too. First thing tomorrow."

"That should be easy enough," said Dennis, deep in his tourist's guide to Germany. "They seem mad on footwear over there. They don't have pounds and pence like us – you have to pay for everything in Doc Martens."

"DMs means *Deutschmarks*, dummy!" sighed Benny. "Now let's get ourselves aboard this flippin' German plane and see what film they're showing."

Luke had an aisle seat next to Frederick. The Cool Ruler of Albion's defence had none of Luke's problems in getting away for games. He lived with his elder sister and kept whatever hours he chose. That often involved taking days off school to run his rare records search business. Since he already knew more than most of his subject-teachers, no one saw any point in complaining.

"Hey, Exchange Man," he murmured as Luke fastened his seat-belt. "Bummer that you can't chill in the hotel with the rest of us."

Luke shrugged. "I've got to stay with these friends of the head in case my mum rings to check up on me. But they sound like OK people, the Sturms."

"There's a young *frä*
raised an eyebrow behind

"I've got no idea. Ursula, i
know a thing about her."

Just then, as the plane took off,
broke out behind Luke and Frederick.
got hold of Chrissie's passport and, in   of
the young slaphead's desperate attempts to
stop him, he was now holding up the photo for
everyone else to whistle and jeer at. Or rather:
the *photos*. For although Chrissie's head was
now snooker-ball smooth, he'd once been
proudly known as The Boy With The Biggest
Hair In The Nationwide League. So big, in fact,
that he'd needed two photos from a booth to
get it all in.

The fun ended as a *Lufthansa* stewardess
plucked the passport from Narris's hand and
returned it to Chrissie. "I think it's a very *nice*
photo, Herr Pick," Luke heard her whisper,
fluttering her eyelashes at the Supermodels'
Choice.

"What does she mean *Hair* Pick?" Chrissie
muttered. "Is she winding me up?"

Then, as the plane climbed, the captain intro-
duced himself over the intercom and wished
everyone a pleasant flight.

"As some of you may by now have noticed,"
he went on in textbook English, "we have
the pleasure today of flying the Castle Albion

squad to *Franz-Josef-Strauss-Flughafen* Munich." There was some polite applause (and one or two boos from Man U fans who still hadn't got over that FA Cup Final defeat). "We wish Albion the best of luck in their UEFA Cup tie against mighty Bayern, who – incidentally – hold a one-nil advantage from the first leg in England. I hope it is a match to remember in the Olympiastadion. May the best team win. Just remember, Herr Webb and all you players: in Europe, away goals count double!"

Luke saw Carl look puzzled at that. He was sitting across the aisle from Luke, next to Craig and Dennis who were furiously scribbling away at their novel. "Away goals count double," Carl was mouthing and shaking his head.

"What's up, Carl?" Luke asked.

"It's that away-goal rule," said the big striker. "I've never really understood it. I mean, are we *two*-nil down now, or is it just one?"

"No, no," grinned Luke. "The away goals only count double if it's a draw, on aggregate, at the end of the second leg."

Carl looked at him. "Right," he said slowly. "On *aggregate*. Right."

"If it's *not* a draw after the second leg," Luke went on, "the away goals don't count double at all. Well, they don't have to then, do they?"

"No, I guess they don't," Carl half-smiled,

nodding now. "Cheers, Luke." He still looked absolutely baffled, but Luke couldn't see how else to explain it.

After half an hour in the air, Benny came up and squatted down between them. "It's smashin' to have you with us for an away leg, Luke," he said. "And just before we left, I had a call from Terry too. He's managed to hook up with Dogan somewhere in the Czech Republic. If we keep our fingers crossed, they *should* get to Munich just in time for the game on Wednesday night." He lowered his voice in case any of the German staff could hear. "So with you playin', and the Dog up front, I really reckon we can nick a result over there."

Luke smiled at him. You had to hand it to the Big Bossman. He never gave up hope. How many other managers could watch their team go down at Swansea and still think they had a chance days later against Bayern? Or maybe it was just plain desperation now? *Heads will roll*, Jimbo had said. Poor, poor Benny.

"The family you're staying with live just a few minutes from our hotel," he went on. "Your headmistress really did us proud on that one. I wish *I* was staying with a nice little family, instead of having to chase round after this rotten lot morning, noon and night. I'm telling you: it's like looking after an army of toddlers.

You've got the best deal here, Luke, no sweat."
Suddenly he shot to his feet. "Oi! Chrissie!" he
yelled. "Give Keith his trousers back!"

18

The airport in Munich was a gleaming, state-of-the-art affair. All the Albion squad sailed through customs. Only Benny was stopped – but that was just because an official wanted to admire his sheepskin coat at closer quarters.

Herr and *Frau* Sturm were waiting in Arrivals – a small, smartly-dressed, friendly-looking pair. Luke knew who they were because they were holding up a card with "HEADLESS HERO" written on it.

"We are sorry about these words," Frau Sturm said with a blush to Benny. "Luke's head-mistress, our dear old friend, suggested them. She thought that if we wrote 'Luke Green', it would only attract hordes of his many fans."

"He is extremely popular over here," Herr Sturm smiled, taking Luke's bag. "And, of course, in Germany there is no ban on showing his face in magazines or on advertisement posters. So nobody knows him here as 'Headless Hero'."

"Right you are then," said Benny. "Well, I'll

leave you in the capable hands of these folks, Luke. And I'll be round at nine in the morning so we can go on our little shopping expedition." He grinned, raised one foot and tapped his shoe.

Herr Sturm hadn't been kidding about Luke's popularity. On their way to the car park no fewer than fourteen people said hello to him, saluted, or wished him good luck for Wednesday – "But not *too* good, eh!" each of them added.

"Castle Albion have many admirers in Munich," Herr Sturm told Luke as they sped away towards town. "*Ach*, any team that beats Man United in a Cup Final is fine by us! But on Wednesday, I am afraid, we must cheer for Bayern. Well, most of us, anyway." He winked, although Luke wasn't quite sure why.

He smiled back and nodded, staring out of the window. He loved arriving in foreign countries at night. At first, around the airports, you could hardly see anything. Then the street lights would start to twinkle, and neon signs in weird languages would give you a taste of what was to come. Then in the morning you'd wake to find a whole new city around you – just waiting to be explored.

Frau Sturm was giving him a potted history of the city – mentioning various landmarks that he probably wouldn't have time to see. But

Luke wasn't too bothered that he wouldn't get to tour the BMW works, or visit Nymphenburg Palace, or take a stroll through the famous English Garden.

The place he was always keenest to see in any foreign city was the football ground. Which, here in Munich, also meant seeing the vast stadium complex built around it for the 1972 Olympic Games. And Luke wasn't just going to take a peek at *that* like a tourist. Tomorrow afternoon he would be training on the fabulous pitch, while on Wednesday night he would be *playing* on it! To be honest, trainer trouble apart, he really couldn't have asked for much more.

"And this now is the district of Schwabing, in which we live," Herr Sturm said, waving out at trendy-looking streets full of cafés, bars and restaurants. "Ursula will probably be waiting at the window of our flat. She is very excited at the prospect of your visit, Luke. But alas, she is a very shy girl."

"She will probably not pluck up the courage to speak with you until it is time for you to leave!" Frau Sturm went on. "But she is a terribly big fan of yours, believe me. And she is almost exactly the same age as you too. There, see! There she is! There is our dear Ursula!"

Luke looked up at the high window where she was pointing. But all he saw was a swish of long, golden hair before the curtains closed, hiding her from view.

"What did I tell you?" laughed Herr Sturm. "She is too shy even to wave!"

"Right," said Luke, nodding. That swish of golden hair had impressed him. Just like a princess in some old German fairytale. And she was a "terribly big fan" of his too. Maybe this would turn into an even better trip than he'd expected...

There was no sign of Ursula as the Sturms showed Luke to his neat and comfortable room in the spacious flat. After he'd unpacked, and Frau Sturm had brought him a mug of delicious hot chocolate, Herr Sturm asked if he would like to phone home – "Just to announce that you have arrived safely".

"OK," smiled Luke.

"If we may, we will speak briefly to your mother first," said Herr Sturm. "To reassure her that you are quite safe with us." He frowned. "We do not *like* to deceive her in this way over the UEFA match, but your headmistress says that her hatred of football is quite mad and unreasonable. And besides, anyone with a God-given talent such as yours should be allowed to display it. I will ring."

Moments later, Luke heard the Sturms listing to his mum all the things he would be doing over the next two days. (Or rather, the things he *would* have been doing, if he hadn't had a massive match to prepare for and play in.) Then Frau Sturm called him out to the phone in the hallway.

"Hello, Mum," he said, as the Sturms shut themselves into their kitchen to give him some privacy. "It's brilliant here. Fantastic. Great place."

"Have you got your new shoes on?" she asked, ignoring all that.

"Sorry?"

"Your new black shoes – have you got them on? I don't want to think of you slobbing around in your socks like you do here. You're a *guest*, remember."

"Yes, Mum." He looked down and wriggled his toes. He wasn't even wearing his socks. He'd taken them off too. There were blisters all over his feet from the ill-fitting shoes. "Have you heard from Nan and Grandpa at all?" Luke asked. He was still bothered about Vealy's flight arrangements; he really couldn't see why they'd had to go to Hamburg first, instead of flying straight to Munich. "I was just wondering how *they* were getting on over here."

"Oh, I haven't heard a thing from them. Far too busy enjoying themselves to phone *me*." She snorted. "Anyway – how are you getting on with the girl there? Speaking lots of German to her, I hope. You'd better be."

Luke realized then that he hadn't spoken a single word of German since he'd arrived. He also realized that the door marked URSULA along the hall had come fractionally open. He couldn't *see* anyone watching him, but he sensed it.

"Oh – er – we're getting on like a house on fire," Luke told his mum. "Better go now. This call must be costing a fortune. Speak to you later."

As soon as he put down the phone, Frau Sturm called him to the kitchen, where she'd prepared a feast for the three of them: cold meats and sausages, a baker's display of bread rolls, huge piles of dumplings and salads and noodles...

"Wow!" gaped Luke. "But isn't Ursula going to join us?"

"No, no," beamed Herr Sturm. "Ursula has very little interest in food. You know how it is with young girls? Forever fretting about their figures!"

Luke smiled, then tucked in and forgot all about the shy, golden-haired girl for a while. But when bedtime came around, she still hadn't put in an appearance. Luke said goodnight to her parents, took a quick shower, and hopped into bed. It had been a busy day. Soon he was sound asleep.

But twice before morning he woke up

suddenly. Both times, he felt sure he'd heard his door being opened. Both times he then thought he heard quick footsteps, and a door *closing* further down the hall. Ursula's door?

No... Surely not?

19

Frau Sturm had laid on another belter of a spread for breakfast. "I believe my good wife wishes for you to eat so much," Herr Sturm explained, "that you will not be able to run at the Olympiastadion tomorrow evening!"

Luke laughed and dug in anyway. "Ursula had to leave early for her school," said her mother. "Tonight, we hope, she will be brave enough to meet you!"

"Yes, that would be good," said Luke through a mouthful of Pumpernickel bread – wondering now if he had just dreamed those disturbances in the night. But he also noticed that there were no photos of the fräulein – anywhere.

At nine on the dot, Benny Webb turned up accompanied by a young, off-duty beautician from his hotel. "Mariella here is going to show us where we can get hold of some trainers for you," Benny told Luke. "Oh, and a pineapple for Carl. Phew, the bother I had with our lot last night! It's a blinkin' relief to get away and let

Ruel look after 'em for a couple of hours. Half of them had a fire-extinguisher fight at three o'clock in the mornin'. And that was *before* the other half got back from some nightclub Frederick took 'em all out to."

Mariella's eyes lit up at the mention of Cool F's name. "He is a very splendid dancer, your friend Friedrich," she told Luke. "My, what a mover! He floats like a moth and stings like a wasp – isn't that what you say in English?"

"Something like that," Luke nodded.

"We have called a cab for you," said Herr Sturm, as boss, boy and beautician left the flat. "Have a happy day, Luke. And tonight," he winked, "we very much hope that you will finally meet our nervous little Ursula."

"Well," said Benny in the cab, "At last there's been a bit of good news. Dog and Tel are now cycling across German soil – and they should be here in time for the big kick-off tomorrow. I got a call from Vealy this morning."

"Vealy?"

"Yeah, he's the Dog's agent, see. He's been with the two of them for the past couple of days. Drivin' behind 'em in some sort of hire-car, as I understand it."

"He didn't mention my nan and grandpa, did he?" asked Luke. "He's meant to have fixed them up with a flight to the game. But you know what Vealo's like. You don't happen to know anything about it, do you?"

Benny pulled a face and scratched his great fizz of grey hair. "Now that you bring it up, he *did* say something about your olds to me – before we left England." He closed his eyes and racked his brain to remember. "Somethin', as I recall, about them being part of the pre-match entertainment..."

"*What!*"

Benny shook his head. "Sorry, son. That's all he told me. But he said it was well in hand. I shouldn't worry yourself about it. Not yet anyway." Wearily he nudged Luke in the ribs – this guy had three A levels and a degree in worrying.

"Here we are now," cried Mariella. "This is where we get out for pineapples!"

Finding a pineapple was a breeze. Finding Luke the right footwear was not. Mariella took them to one shop after another. Each offered a stunning array of trainers in every brand known to man. But not a single store had a pair just like Luke's old ones. And that was what he wanted. What he needed. However hard Mariella tried to describe them to the assistants, nobody could help.

"They must've stopped making 'em," sighed Benny in the end. "Look, son. Just pick the best pair you can find for now." He pointed at his watch. "We really should be getting up to the stadium for training. I've left poor old Ruel in charge of that bunch of prannets for way too long already."

Luke chose a fabulous (and fabulously expensive) pair of white Nikes – which the store-manager wouldn't dream of letting Benny pay for: "It is an *honour* for us to provide soccer shoes for the Studless Sensation, Herr Webb! Just as long as he does not use one to score a goal against Bayern! No, no – I merely joke!"

Luke was a bit down on the longish drive to the Olympiastadion. These new trainers were bound to give him blisters as he broke them in. And he already had all those blisters from the vile black shoes. It wasn't ideal. His only real hope now lay with Rodney. Maybe his stepdad did have some sort of plan for getting his old trainers back, but Luke rather doubted it. And then, on top of that, there were his grandparents to worry about. *Pre-match entertainment* indeed!

But when they reached their destination – the legendary Bayern ground with its amazing glass roof that pitched up like an enormous tent – he forgot about his feet and the old folks for a while. Quickly he got changed, then out he went on to the grass to join the rest of the Albion squad in their gaping wonderment.

"This must all be a dream," breathed Half-Fat. "Pinch me, someone."

Which, quite naturally, Madman did – very hard – on the back of the midfield man's neck. At once the two Albion players fell to the ground in quite a meaty scuffle – in front of the massed ranks of the world's press invited in to witness the session. It didn't look good. "Stop it! *Stop* that!" screamed an all-too-familiar voice. "I will *not* have behaviour like this, do you hear me!"

Benny came up alongside Luke to watch as a small person in a number ten shirt – the owner of the voice and a whole lot else besides – tried with all his might to tug Half-Fat off Madman. "Yeah, right," the boss muttered. "I never got around to tellin' you the bad news in the taxi. Jimbo's arrived, and he's raring to play."

"Never mind," Chrissie came up and whispered. "Maybe we can put him on the injured list now. A little mistimed tackle? An accidental clash of heads?"

"*No* more brawling!" JP was screaming louder than ever, as he finally prised Half-Fat off. "We're guests in this magnificent stadium, for heaven's sake!"

He turned, put his hands on his hips and addressed the whole squad. "Not *one* of you will touch so much as a hair on another player's head for the whole of the rest of this session. No contact! Absolutely *no* contact! Any offender will be sent *straight* back to England on my own plane! *IS THAT CLEAR?*"

"Oh well," said Chrissie under his breath. "That's that idea out of the window."

"Right," cried Benny, clapping his hands. "Let's start with twenty laps."

As usual the players ran off in pairs. Luke found himself next to Carl.

"Oh, Luke," he frowned, "I've been wanting to ask you something." He glanced around and lowered his voice. "It's just that I was wondering: when you're away from home, how many goals do you have to score to get a hat-trick...?"

20

All things considered, it was a good session. Jimbo's no-contact ruling made a bit of a horlicks of Benny's full-scale match at the finish. But before then everyone put in some pretty solid fitness work. And the set-piece rehearsals went well (as long as the player-chairman was persuaded to stand well clear). Frederick, rather than a slightly-puzzled Luke, was detailed to take all the practice free-kicks and corners, and a very fine job he made of them too.

When Benny called a halt, the media men and women applauded Albion off the pitch. The boss gave them a few well-chosen soundbites to put in their reports, then caught up with the players for a team-talk after they'd showered.

"Right lads," Mr Sheepskin said. "I think we've pulled the wool over their eyes with that. We'll use *none* of those set-piece moves tomorrow night, right? They'll all be writing about *Frederick* the dead-ball expert now. And that's what Bayern will be expecting. But once the match starts, we go back to our usual game-plan – with *Luke* taking everything. OK?" He tapped his head. "At this level of European competition, you've always got to be one step ahead of the enemy." Then he glanced at Luke, who was massaging his bare feet. "New trainers all right there, Studless?" he asked.

"Um ... ye-es," replied Luke. But everyone could see he had blisters on his blisters. And out on the pitch he hadn't been quite his usual twinkle-toed self.

Benny stared at him. "It'll all come right on the night, son. You'll see."

After another hour of in-depth tactical discussion, the players headed back to their hotel for dinner – and a cab arrived to whisk Luke home to the Sturms. As soon as he arrived, his mum rang up and quizzed him for a full sixty minutes. It wasn't easy to give a graphic account of how he'd spent the day as a guest-pupil at Ursula's school. He made a far better job of describing the Marienplatz shopping centre – where Ursula had "taken him at lunchtime". What he really wanted was to speak with Rod and see if he'd had any luck on the trainer front. But apparently he was out up a tree somewhere, looking at owls.

At last Luke wrenched himself free, to be rewarded with another slap-up Sturm meal. Yet again, the young lady of the house was nowhere to be seen. But this time when Luke patted his stomach, bloated, Frau Sturm had a surprise in store.

"Now Luke," she smiled broadly. "The moment has arrived. Ursula feels that she is ready to greet you. She waits for you in her room."

"Along you go," added Herr Sturm. "She is expecting you. Just remember: she is normally dreadfully shy with boys – yet she is *very* keen on you!"

Luke got up slowly from the table. The dapper little couple beamed at him and nodded. They looked so normal, so *nice*. So what *was* it with this daughter of theirs?

He trudged out into the hall on his stinging feet. At the end of it he could see Ursula's door was now slightly ajar. A dim, red light was on inside. The closer he came, a faint sound of music grew louder. He knew that vocal.

Velvet geraniums rise from the sea
Turning the night into da-ay.
Watch for the duck in the stone limousine
START TO PRAY...!

It was Luke's dad. Singing "Castle Rap" – the Albion Cup Final single that had catapulted him to major-league fame back in May. Softly, he knocked on the door. There was no answer. He knocked again, a bit louder. Still no answer.

He knocked a third time, this time nudging the door back another couple of inches.

At that moment the single finished playing, and a tiny voice said, "*Komm.*"

Luke felt his heart rise as he grabbed the door-handle and took a single step forward. This was it. The moment of truth. In the dusky red light, he felt as if *he* was now entering a fairy tale. He swung his eyes around the room, half-expecting to find a beautiful young princess working away at a spinning-wheel.

But that's not what he saw. Instead, his eyes popped as he took in all four walls. Almost every inch was covered with pages torn from news-papers, magazines and football programmes. And every single picture on them was of *him*! She'd drawn pictures of her own as well. Again, all of him. In Albion kit, in school clothes – even, oh wow, in swimming trunks on a beach.

Then Luke finally saw her: over in the corner – golden hair in braids above a floor-length blue dress, and gaping at him in awe. Gaping *down* at him. Luke blinked. Then he looked harder. She was enormous! Not fat, exactly. Not really fat at all. "Big-boned", his nan would have called it. She was absolutely mountainous. As if one of the Alps had done a runner and wound up in here.

"Luke Green!" she squeaked. "*The* Luke Green! I think that maybe I shall die!"

Luke gulped. Then he waved. "Hi, Ursula. Great to meet you."

"Call me Uschi," she said coyly, letting a plait of hair fall across one eye.

For what seemed like an eternity they gazed at each other in disbelief. Then the gigantic German girl fluttered her eyelashes. *Shy?* From where Luke was standing, she looked about as shy as Madman sitting down to cod and chips for five. Obviously she was making a very special effort in his honour.

"Oh Luke," she gasped. "I am your number one fan! Do please come in. And close the door behind you. I do not want my parents to be disturbed by our noise. Oh Studless Sensation, we have *such* an evening ahead of us..."

Two and a half hours later, Luke emerged and staggered down the hall to his room – more exhausted than he'd been after any training session. He'd never known anything like it. Big Uschi just couldn't get enough.

She would have made him stay even longer too. But luckily he convinced her that he needed some sleep before his big game. Even so, she made him promise that they would pick up tomorrow night at the exact point where they'd left off.

Which was halfway through the previous season's Cup semi-final between Albion and

Arsenal. Uschi had *begged* him for a blow-by-blow account of every game in Albion's historic FA Cup run. She'd seen the video highlights (and knew them off by heart) but what she wanted now was Luke's own view.

Not only that. She got him to act out certain moves as well: his cross for Ruel to head home against Aston Villa; his own equalizer against Newcastle; his corner which led to Frederick's winner at Wolves. The girl was insatiable. She was hungry for detail about Albion's last two League seasons too. "Describe to me the layout of the Victoria Ground, Hartlepool," she would say between re-enactments of the Cup matches. "What was it like to go down at home to lowly Scarborough?" "Just how tense was that relegation decider with Exeter?"

It was all pretty strange, but in a way Luke enjoyed it almost as much as she did. He fell asleep as soon as his head hit the pillow, with a big tired smile on his face.

Now was that a true fan, he thought, just before conking out, *or what*?

21

It was six forty-five – an hour to go to the big kick-off. In the ultra-plush VIP lounge at the Olympiastadion, Bayern officials and former players were lavishing hospitality on Albion's special guests for the evening.

These guests were a pretty mixed bunch. They ranged from old Mrs Bowman, tea-lady at Ash Acre since 1957, and Jimbo's lovely young personal assistant Estella, to Rocky Mitford with a handful of his Southsiders – plus Herr Sturm, who was decked out in Bayern's grey, and Uschi the Alp, proudly festooned in an Albion cap and scarf over an enormous anorak.

Under Jimbo's orders, the squad put in an appearance too. On the way up, Benny warned Madman that if he even *looked* at any of the heaps of snacks on offer, he would lose a week's wages. No one, though, could stop JP from striking business deals with just about every German he shook hands with.

Luke kept moving round the room, meeting

and greeting his local fans. But everywhere he went, Uschi was always just two steps behind. And he could almost feel her fan-in-heaven's smile burning into his back. True enough, she was shy. If anyone else said a word to her, she would shrivel up on the spot. But every time she made eye-contact with Luke, the floodgates would open. "Talk to me about your second goal against Brighton in October," she gushed one time. "Do you prefer to play in long- or short-sleeved shirts?" she cooed. "Is roast chicken still your favourite pre-match meal?" she simpered.

Chrissie overheard and rolled his eyes at Luke. He knew *all* about over-eager young women. But you could have fitted three of his catwalk cuties into Big Uschi here. And although Luke liked her, and he appreciated her interest, he couldn't shake her off. It was as if she had him on a lead – like a pet dachshund.

Soon all the other players saw what was going on. They thought it was an absolute hoot. Carl popped up on Luke's left and hissed, "Tell mc, Studless, may I lick your trainers clean after the game?" Then Madman popped up on his right and whispered, "*Please* can I have the clippings from your next haircut?"

But Benny Webb noticed nothing at all. He'd long ago stopped stealing glances at his watch. Now he just stared at it constantly –

counting off the seconds, cursing himself for ever having got involved with an Armenian sheep-farmer.

"Still no word from the bike boys, then?" Craig asked him.

"Not a sausage," spluttered Big Ben. "I'll have that Veal's guts for garters. He hasn't rung me since Landshut, and I can't get him on *his* mobile at all."

"So what you gonna do, Boss?" asked Narris with a glimmer of hope in his eye. Benny had already broken the news that he would be on the bench that night. Albion would then put out a three-man midfield, and bravely field three strikers: Carl, the Dog ... and Jimbo. "Does this mean I'm back in?"

"As of this minute, son, yes you are." Benny growled. "Oh, I'll put that Veal in a crate!" He sounded furious but Luke had never seen him look more forlorn. It wasn't hard to see why. His job was right on the line, yet here he was – going into this super-tricky fixture without his new matchwinner but *with* matchloser James Prince. He clapped his hands. "OK, my lot – time we got changed. Thank you kindly, sirs and madams, for entertaining us. Now Albion – follow me." He marched out of the lounge at the head of his troops.

"Good luck," Uschi purred as Luke bade her farewell. "Although you will not need it. A player of your class makes his own luck. Tell me though, *are* you superstitious...?"

Did she never give it a rest? Luke smiled, shrugged, and was glad to let Gaffer lead him away without another word. On the way to the dressing room, he looked hard for his nan and grandpa. They had been invited to the VIP knees-up too. But there was no more sign of them than there was of Dog, Tel or Vealy. *Pre-match entertainment*, Luke thought every time he passed a wall-mounted TV-set showing live closed-circuit pictures from the already-packed stadium. All he could see were tiny kids playing on a shortened pitch. And all he could feel, as he trudged after Benny, were the blisters his new trainers had given him at training that morning.

"Here, hold on a minute, Boss," Gaffer cried as they entered the last carpeted corridor leading down to the dressing room. "What's this?"

Benny turned and looked down at the skirting-board where Gaffer was pointing. Quick as a flash, Craig stooped and scooped up a small, round-ish black thing. He held it out for everyone to see. "It's one of those clips cyclists wear. To stop the bottoms of their trousers getting caught up in their bike chains!"

"And here's another one!" called Dennis, rushing on ahead.

"And look," yelled Half-Fat, charging almost as far as the dressing-room door. "There's this too!" He bent down, then came up brandishing a bicycle pump.

A slow smile spread across everyone's faces, except poor old Narris'.

"Oh please God," murmured Benny with his eyes shut, "let this be the Dog."

At that, the dressing-room door was torn back and Terry V's head popped out. "*There* you all are!" he grinned. "We was wondering if you'd gone home!"

"Thank you, God!" beamed Benny, his eyes still shut tight.

"Well, come on in, the lot of you," said Terry. "Meet your new team-mate!"

In they all charged, shoving Terry aside, to get a look at the legendary marksman that all of them – including Benny – had only ever seen on video.

And there he was! Mezir the Magician! Standing tall and dark and proud in the dressing room, already in his boots and number-nine Albion shirt. Luke blinked. He'd never seen such muscular legs in all his life. Clearly over the years this guy had biked a *lot* of miles. Who needed powered transport? From the look of him, he could easily have out-run TAFKAG's van or Rodney's Ford Escort.

Without any introductions, Benny hurled himself at the Armenian goal-machine and hugged him so hard that Ruel had to tug him off in case he accidentally crippled the goal-ace. Then each player in turn bounced up and shook the grinning Dogman's hand, while Terry reeled off their names for him.

He said nothing at all until Luke, the last up, gave him a shake. Then the Major Talent from Asia Minor raised both hands, palms out, and said in a floor-shakingly deep voice: "I am exceedingly pleased to meet you."

"Wow!" gasped Carl. "You can speak English too!"

"And better than you can, Carl!" quipped Chrissie.

Dogan smiled a big moustachioed smile at both of them. "I am *exceedingly* pleased to meet you," he repeated – clearly speaking from the heart.

"Well, we're all exceedingly pleased too, old son," Gaffer told him.

"So are you up for it?" asked Narris, trying to hide his disappointment at finding himself back on the bench. "You're not too tired after your long ride?"

Dog widened his already big eyes at Phizo, and nodded his head. "I am exceedingly *pleased*," he told him as if his life depended on it, "to meet you."

At that, the dressing room went a fair bit quieter. The truth had started to dawn. "Hey

Dog," called Madman. "What's the name of the Queen's husband?"

He turned to face the keeper. "I am exceedingly," he said, "pleased to meet *you*."

"OK," said Terry, stepping in quickly – and *his* legs under his shorts were rippling with new muscles too. "As you may have noticed, our Dog's got a fairly limited vocabulary – as yet. But he's learning all the time. Before you know it, he'll be telling the whole world, 'Well it's a game of two halves, but at the end of the day it's all about taking your chances'."

"He'll be as right as ninepence," agreed Benny. "Now, this is where our season is *really* gonna slip into gear. So get changed the rest of you. You've got a little date with destiny in about," he looked at his watch, "thirty minutes time!"

22

With everyone else changed, Luke was putting plasters on his blisters when the dressing-room door opened. A Raybanned, gelled-up head popped round it.

"*Ciao*, lads!" cried Vealy. "Just wanted to wish you all the best. Go get 'em!" He glanced over his shoulder, then said in a lower voice to Dogan. "They say every dog has his day. Well, I reckon this one's gonna be yours, old buddy!"

Dog smiled dazzlingly. "I *am* exceedingly pleased to meet you!" he cried.

Then the agent looked Luke's way and frowned. "Spot of bother with the old footwear, then, Studless?"

"No, the *new* footwear," muttered Luke. "I'd give anything to have my old trainers back for this game. I don't think I'll be standing after ten minutes." Then he looked up. "And hey – what have you done with my grandparents?"

At that, Veal winked. Only a special kind of

person can make a wink work behind sun-glasses. But Agent Veal was one of those people. "Tell you what, Lukey," he purred. "Reckon I've got just the thing for you out here." He jerked his head backwards. "If I could have only a *minute* of your time..." Then he disappeared again.

"My nan and grandpa?" gasped Luke, jump-ing up from the bench and hobbling across the dressing-room floor before Benny could order him to stay put. "Are they *here*? Have you brought them down to see me?" He didn't push any of the other players out of the way. He wasn't big enough for that. But Chrissie, Dennis and Keats Aberdeen all stepped pretty briskly aside. Only Jimbo didn't see the barefooted young midfielder coming. And vice-versa.

Flanked by two minders, the player-chairman had wandered in front of the door trying to get a better signal on his mobile. Luke, seeing only the door-handle, cannoned straight into him – sending JP sprawling and his mobile looping up in the air to be caught by one sure-fingered minder. "Hey!" screeched Princey.

"Oh, sorry," Luke panted, without looking back. He was already out of the door.

The next ten seconds changed everything. For Luke, for Albion, for everyone. Only ten seconds. But it seemed like a whole lot longer. So *much* happened.

As soon as Luke got outside, he found Vealy standing just down the long corridor to his right – smirking fit to burst. "I think *this* is what you're looking for," he grinned. He nodded towards a point further down the corridor.

Luke took a few steps in that direction, then – smelling smoke – he paused and blinked. For a moment he couldn't make sense of it. He had fully expected to see his nan and grandpa coming towards him. Instead, the corridor was almost blocked by another fast-approaching figure: Uschi!

Here we go *again*, thought Luke – beginning to wonder if she planned to come back to England with him after the game and set up camp in his garden.

When she saw her hero she beamed, and held out a brown-paper parcel that she was carrying in both hands. "It is for you," she cried. "It was delivered to my home, and mother has brought it here! It says Very Urgent upon it!"

But Veal hadn't been nodding at Uschi. She had just come on the scene – surging past two figures that Luke could now just see behind her. Two men in white coats – one of whom was shouting, "Hello..." But this time he didn't get as far as "...Headless Hero!" Suddenly the reek of smoke got much stronger. And then, without warning, there was a bright flash and an almighty bang.

There went the *Lukewarm Mark Fives*!

Veal hurled himself to the floor, Luke pressed himself back against the corridor wall. And Uschi gave a little shriek of panic before hurtling forward.

She was really motoring as she passed Luke but she still managed to stuff the parcel safely into his hands. Then the weirdest thing of all happened.

Just at that moment, Jimbo tore back the dressing-room door and stomped out into the corridor. He'd dusted himself down from the knock Luke had given him. Now his blood was up and he wanted a serious word with the boy wonder.

"*Luke!*" he began, turning to the right – only to meet the full force of the stampeding Uschi. Luke, Veal and the boffins looked on in horror.

The first explosion had been bad. This one was worse. Luke had heard of someone coming down like a ton of bricks on somebody else. Uschi coming down on top of Princey was like the fall of the Berlin Wall. And it happened so fast! One moment she was going full pelt. The next she was flat out on the carpet. *Really* flat. As Luke, Veal and the boffins took several steps on tiptoe towards the scene of the crash, there was no sign at all of the player-chairman.

Bayern officials came rushing up too. And Terry V bolted out of the Albion dressing-room to see what was up (or down) – followed by Benny and the lads.

"Let me through!" Terry yelled. "I'm a doctor!" A physio *is* a doctor ... sort of.

A handful of players helped Uschi to her feet. "I am OK, I am OK," she kept saying, twisting around to check out Princey. "*Ach*, I could have fallen on Luke, I could have crushed Studless Sensation... Oh, but how is Herr Prince?"

Splattered, was the answer to that. He seemed to be imprinted into the floor: both arms out, both knees knocked, both lenses smashed in his glasses. But he was breathing – and groaning – very faintly. Tel knelt down beside him. And even before he took a proper look at him, he solemnly pronounced, "I'm afraid there is no question whatever of this man playing football tonight."

"There never was!" Luke heard Craig whisper to Dennis, who giggled.

"Would you not like a second opinion?" asked a white-haired old German, kneeling on JP's other side. "I too am a doctor. To me, he looks only winded."

Terry eyeballed the old guy. "There is *no question* of this man playing tonight!" he repeated through gritted teeth. "What he needs is painkillers, and a good long rest. Lads – get him back inside. Oh, and Narris – get changed, son."

Back in the dressing room, a groggy Jimbo tried to protest his fitness. But Terry and Ruel managed to convince him that he'd broken at least one rib. "I just can't risk you out there, Jimbo lad," Benny told him with a sombre look. "However vital you are to this team, *your health has to come first.*"

Everyone else could hardly stop themselves from whooping with joy. Jimbo was out! Narris was in! The Dog was up front! And Luke – well, Luke had no more problems now about what to wear on his feet that night. It was a miracle! Rodney had done the business for him after all! Oh bow-wow-*wow*!

For, amid all the chaos, he had unwrapped Uschi's parcel and found inside ... his dear old trainers! They smelled a bit fishy but otherwise they were in tip-top condition. *Found these in the bins at the back of the shoe shop*, said a scribbled note from his stepdad. *Hope you find a use for them!* Magic, magic, magic! As soon as Luke slipped them on, it felt as if he'd scored ten away goals.

"Right lads!" bellowed Benny – already looking a lot more like the Sheepskin Supremo of old. "No time for a team-talk. You don't need one anyway. Not now. Just remember what I said before the home leg. BARK!"

"Woof-woof!" went Gaffer. "Woof-woof-*woof*!" added Half-Fat. "Woof-woof-woof-

woof-*woof*!" Chrissie joined in. And soon everyone except Luke and a baffled-looking Armenian ex-shepherd was yapping the house down.

Luke wiggled his toes in the world's best pair of trainers and grinned. "Come on, Dog," he shouted. "You know how to bark – don't you?" And he did!

23

In the tunnel on the way up to the pitch Luke fell into step with Lothar Matthäus again. "Hey Studless," smiled the super-sweeper. "All that *noise* back there! What are we playing against tonight – a bunch of werewolves?"

"You wait till we get our teeth into you!" Luke smiled back, walking on air in his old trainers. He had *such* a good feeling about the next ninety minutes. And, to be fair, the Albion din was nothing like what he was hearing up ahead. Not just from the frenzied 60,000-plus crowd, but also from a helicopter high over the stadium, from which a whole football team of parachutists was sailing down on to the grass. Now *that* was what Luke called pre-match entertainment.

"*Ach,*" Matthäus yelled above the uproar as they waited for all the jumpers to make their landings. He was still chuckling at the earlier barking. "I think all you English are quite mad! I mean, just look at your grandparents there."

"My *what*?" boomed Luke.

"Why, your grandpapa and grandmama. Surely you knew? There was a page all about them in the match programme. But I suppose you do not read German?"

"I... I..." Luke croaked, but he couldn't move his mouth to say anything else.

He was staring past the floodlights into the black night sky, up where Matthäus was pointing. Nine of the jumpers were on the grass by now, their Bayern-grey parachutes collapsing around them. The last two finally floated into view. Close together. *So* close that they appeared to be joined. They *were* joined. Luke could see that each of them was holding the end of a banner.

"Oh," said Luke very softly. "Oh, oh..."

The parachutes of these last two jumpers had broad blue-and-white hoops. The letters on their banner were blue-on-white too. Suddenly they became legible:

Good Luck, Luke – Our Top Grandson!

"Oh..." was all Luke could continue to say as both his nan and grandpa made perfect descents into the centre-circle, then stood to take wild applause from the crowd. Glancing at the screen, Luke saw their thrilled faces in close-up. These people were seventy years old! Mad, Matthäus had said. Quite, *quite* mad.

But now at least he knew that they were safe.

And they were here, after all, just to watch him. After what they'd put themselves through, he *had* to play a blinder. For them, for Benny, for Rocky and the travelling Southsiders ... for everyone. When the ref then signalled for the players to run out on to the cleared pitch, Luke raced on so fast that his trainers felt turbo-charged.

Was this young man up for the biggest game of his life so far? Just a little!

Even though vastly outnumbered, Rocky and his crew gave the Dog a rousing welcome. They chanted his name all through the kick-in, then unfurled a great Union flag banner with LOVE ME, LOVE MY DOG printed across it. The brand-new striker was clearly moved. If Gaffer hadn't grabbed him on his way back from tossing up, he would have gone over and said to every single Albion fan in person: "I am exceedingly pleased to meet you!"

And then, as the drums and klaxon horns hit a deafening pitch, Luke couldn't even hear the ref's whistle as the game got under way. This was it. Win or bust.

As ever, as soon as Luke got his first touch of the ball he forgot all about the hugeness of the occasion. And what a touch it was! Cushioning on his thigh a knock-down from Carl just inside the Bayern half, he volleyed a forty-yard pass out to Chrissie who was haring down the left flank. The Pickman swerved around the big defender, Samuel Kuffour, got to the byline, then whipped back a low cross to the edge of the penalty box.

Everyone from Benny to Rocky's five-year-old daughter rolled their eyes in frustration. Chrissie did this *so* often. He got into absolutely brilliant positions, then whacked the ball over without even looking up. There wasn't one Albion man *near* the box. Just four back-pedalling defenders covering the keeper.

But that was when Chrissie *crossed* the ball. A split second later, as the ball sped past the four defenders, someone in a hooped shirt *was* there. Travelling, it seemed, at the speed of light. And not only was he there – he was getting on the end of the pass, and sending in a wickedly spinning left-foot drive towards Kahn's goal. Only a superb reaction-save from the German keeper stopped it from whistling just inside his near post. Sheer Kahn!

Luke blinked. *No one* had smacked in a shot like that for Albion since Ruel's retirement. And even Ruel had never moved so fast to reach one of Chrissie's wayward crosses. The other Albion players swapped wide-eyed glances. All except Dog – for it was he who had unleashed this awesome attempt on goal.

He was clutching his head with both hands in despair. Did this guy set himself high standards or what? Luke was amazed. He'd just hit the shot of the season – yet he was cursing himself for failing to hit the net as well!

But that was only the beginning. For the next half an hour, everyone inside the Olympiastadion was treated to a world premiere of the Dogan Mezir Show. Luke thought he had seen it all when Michael Owen put in that lightning first forty-five against Argentina in World Cup '98. But this was something else again. Dog wasn't as young as Owen (he was twenty-four). He didn't have quite as sharp a haircut (in fact his long black hair looked really pretty messy). But in every other way, he burst on to this scene with *at least* as much impact.

He led the Albion line magnificently. Putting himself about, getting right in amongst the Germans, always presenting a target for his team-mates – who all seemed to be raised to a new level just by his presence. His technique too was quite breathtaking. On the twenty-five-minute mark, Craig took a throw-in to him even though he had Linke *and* Jeremies jockeying him from behind. The Dog simply killed the ball on his forehead, then turned away between them, leaving them both for dead – *with the ball still on his forehead*!

But this was no one-man show. The Amazing Mr Mezir was first and foremost a team player. And at times the Albion camp almost wished he wasn't. In the thirty-fourth minute, then again in the forty-first, he passed to Carl when he had a clear sight of goal himself – and Carl made a dog's breakfast of both shots.

Even so, it wasn't all one-way traffic. No team with Effenberg, Matthäus, Elber, Jeremies and Tarnat in it was likely to sit back and take punishment for a whole half. Although Albion had most of the possession, Bayern posed plenty of threats of their own on the break. Santa Cruz looked just as deadly as he had at Ash Acre. And right on the stroke of half-time, Albion gave him a gilt-edged chance to prove just why he was one of Europe's finest young finishers.

Up till then, Gaffer had been giving a vintage performance. Gone were the days when the veteran centre-back would hoof it over the nearest stand as a first option. Now his passing was as good as anyone's in the team. Several times in the first half he turned defence into attack with a simple, thoughtful ball forward. But now, taking a short throw-out from Madman, he had a *big* blip.

Aiming to stroke the ball out to Luke, he stubbed his toe in the lush turf and rolled it straight towards Santa Cruz. Cool F, his marker, was two steps behind the Paraguayan – but that was two steps too far. Santa Cruz set off like a whippet. The ball stopped dead for him just ten yards outside the box. Without even looking up, he chipped it high towards Madman's far post.

Morty arced himself up and backwards but his desperate one-handed flap was in vain. Santa Cruz had flighted his shot past him with supreme accuracy. But not – as luck would have it – past the post. It thudded against the upright, dropped down, and was caught on the line by a massively grateful Madman.

"Phew!" said Carl to Luke as the half-time whistle went and they trooped off. "Good job *that* didn't go in. We'd never have come back from four down."

"No, no," Luke began. "Not four. Two. It's just *away* goals that count double – and only then if the aggregate scores are level after…" He paused as he saw the cloud of confusion descend over Carl's face again. "Yes, you're right," he decided to smile instead. "Good job it didn't go in!"

24

Benny sent his boys back out with only praise ringing in their ears. "I can't fault you for effort," he said. "And man for man, you're matching them in terms of skill. This is a right humdinger of a European tie and no mistake."

The old Benny was well and truly back. Caught up in the game like this, he was little more than a fan who happened to be sitting in the dugout. Which made him about as much use as Luke's mum at giving tactical advice. Not that the players cared. They rarely understood Benny's tactics anyway. But it was so great to see him bright-eyed and bushy-tailed again that they all ran back out on to the pitch well fired-up for the final forty-five.

In the other dressing room, however, Ottmar Hitzfeld must have pushed all the right buttons for Bayern too. This wasn't the kind of side that sat back on a one-nil aggregate lead and tried to shut the game down. For the next quarter, they went for Albion's jugular. Mehmet Scholl gave

Dennis a particularly torrid time on the flank. Then he switched sides and tormented Craig as well. Effenberg was pulling all the strings in midfield, and Jeremies left poor Half-Fat chasing shadows whenever he upped a gear and honed in on Madman's goal.

But for all their possession, the Germans seldom finished their moves with shots on target. This was mainly because Cool F was marshalling the Albion defence so majestically. The way he kept closing down Elber, Jancker and Santa Cruz, without ever coming close to fouling them, was a wonder to behold. Looking on from further upfield, Luke began to understand why old Alan Hansen had always been so keen on the art of defending. Frederick's positional sense was uncanny, his reading of the game flawless – and when he won the ball, his distribution was a thing of beauty in itself.

So, as the game entered its final phase, the scoresheet remained blank. Third Division Albion were still neck and neck with one of the very top teams in Europe. That was a phenomenal achievement. But – thanks to the goal that Bayern had snatched at Ash Acre – it still wasn't quite enough. Benny's Cup crusaders *had* to grab a goal back if they were going to keep this tie alive.

Benny himself was out of the dugout now: waving, pointing, roaring, stamping – and that was just at the UEFA official who was trying to get him to sit down. Rocky's squadron were giving it their all as well. *Some* lower-league supporters might have settled for a glorious failure against mighty Munich. They might have tried to "enjoy the experience anyway". Not Rocky and Co.

**"You're Just As Good As This Lot!
You're Just As Good As This Lot!
La-la-la-laaa! La-la-la-laaaaa!"**
they assured their on-field heroes.

But to make sure they didn't offend the home fans who outnumbered them so vastly and were generously applauding Albion's efforts, they also threw in a few choruses of

"Stand Up If You Hate Man U!"
– which went down (or rather up) very well.

With support like that, the Albion players couldn't *think* about surrendering. And to be fair, not one of them looked like giving up the ghost. Luke had seen little of the ball since half-time, but he'd probably run further than in three whole League games – chasing, harrying, tackling, covering. Chrissie was backtracking himself into the ground on the other flank. And Muscly Mr Mezir plainly didn't know the meaning of the word "defeat" (along with just about every other word in the English language). You'd never have guessed how far he had cycled to get on that pitch. Dog-tired? This boy was as fit as a fido!

Then it happened. The deadlock was broken – and oh so simply.

It began with Narris humping a hopeful ball deep into Bayern territory. Apart from Kuffour, keeper Kahn was the only player inside his own half. He jogged out of his box and trapped the ball as it rolled harmlessly towards him. Everyone expected him to hoof it straight back where it had come from. They weren't far wrong. Kahn nudged it forward again and glanced up. Elber was waving for it. So was Matthäus, who had been encamped way upfield ever since half-time. Kahn drew back his foot to give it The Big Welly.

But when he swung forward again, he completely failed to make contact. Luke saw it all, full on, and seeing is believing. But this … *this* … was unbelievable. Kahn didn't make an airshot just through poor technique. *There hadn't been anything there for him to kick!* The ball had simply … gone. And the reason it had gone, was that Deadly Dogan had got to it first.

How he did that, neither Luke nor anyone else watching would ever quite be sure. When Kahn shaped up to kick, Dog was in his own half. When Kahn then kicked, Dog materialized in front of him – just like Captain Kirk being beamed down from the Starship *Enterprise*. And not only that. He'd tapped the ball to one side of the keeper, run round the other – and banged home the opener.

"Gooooaaaaalllllllllllllllllll!"

screamed *no one* in the stadium for a split second. It was just too quick. Supernaturally so. But it was real. Real! *Real!* The ball was snug in the back of the net, and Dog was racing towards Rocky's mob, one arm aloft, to celebrate his first strike for the club. Bayern one, Albion one on aggregate! The rest of the visiting team snapped out of their stupor, stormed over to the Dogman and fell on him like an avalanche.

"Nick Nack Paddawack –
Give That Dog A *Bone*!"

hollered the Albion faithful as they too woke up to the wonder of it. Game *on*!

Bayern restarted like zombies. They didn't know what had hit them. And they were clearly scared stiff about being hit again. For the next ten minutes they put Kuffour, Matthäus *and* Lizarazu on Dogan. Everywhere he ran, they dogged his steps – which left some wide-open spaces for the likes of Luke, Carl and Chrissie to make use of. Albion's tails were really wagging now. Luke curled in a cross-shot that bounced on the top of the crossbar. Carl fired in a vicious drive that Kahn scrambled away. Chrissie sent a rare header just wide.

The clock was running down, though. Five minutes to go. Four. If someone didn't score soon, this titanic clash would require extra-time. Hitzfeld was now too nervy for that. From the touchline he waved all his players forward when Bayern next attacked – Matthäus, Kuffour and Lizarazu included. Like any striker worth his salt, Dog trotted back too. He was a *team* man. His duties didn't begin and end with sticking the ball in the opposition's net. He'd already shown he could roll up his sleeves and defend with the best of them.

Scholl was in possession on the right touchline. Dipping a shoulder, he surged past Chrissie before immediately aiming a cross towards Madman's far post. And that's when it all went pear-shaped for Albion...

25

It wasn't deliberate. No one in their right mind could have thought poor old Dog meant to do it. But he found himself in the dock anyway. Just as Kuffour darted forward to get on the end of Scholl's cross, he clipped Dogan's ankle, stumbled, and went sprawling to the ground just inside the box.

The ref can't have been keen on playing extra-time. He blew and pointed at the spot. Albion had given away a pen.

"Oh *no*!" stormed Dennis. "That's *Jimbo's* job!"

And, although all the Albion players surrounded the ref in fury, he wasn't about to change his mind. So now it was all down to Madman – who happened to be just about the best person you could wish for in a situation like this.

In open play, Madman could make as many boo-boos as any dodgy Division Three keeper. And he could be bamboozled by free kicks from almost any distance. But put him twelve yards away from a penalty-taker, and twenty-three times out of twenty-six he would come out on top. That was the number of penalties he'd faced and saved in his professional career. And the last time he'd lost out was three seasons ago.

But a run like that just had to end. And Luke expected it to happen every time the Mad Guy faced a spot-kick. He couldn't help it. Nowadays he couldn't even bear to watch the awful one-on-one take place. Turning away as the Germans debated among themselves who should take it, he saw Benny waving just along the line. "Forward! Get forward, Luke!" he heard. "On halfway! Carl too!" Then he smiled and tapped his head. This was Benny's gesture for: Be Smart.

Luke understood. Being smart in this case meant three things: *expecting* Madman to make the save, *being ready* for a quick throw-out, then *catching Bayern cold* on the break – since any team that has just missed a pen is bound to be all over the place. Luke gave Benny the thumbs up, trotted forward, and waved Carl up alongside him. Still, though, he didn't look back at his own box.

He didn't need to. The crowd's noise told him everything he needed to know. Luke shut his eyes tight. Suddenly the volume fell a little, except from the area around Rocky. That meant the kicker was running in. Then there was a whoosh as 60,000 Germans caught their breath. The ball had been struck. Followed by the sound of 60,000 balloons deflating. *Madman had kept it out!*

Looking at last, Luke saw a host of Bayern players with their heads in their hands. And what was in Madman's hands? The ball? No chance! Already the nutty netminder had hurled it high in Luke's direction. Smart, thought Luke. Very smart. The ball swirled over the heads of the suddenly retreating Bayernets. Before it hit the ground, Luke flicked it further on, spun round, and gave chase at top speed down the right touchline.

The German fans had been stunned into silence by the penalty miss. But Rocky and Co saw distinct possibilities here.

"Go Lukey! Go Lukey!"
they chorused.

Two defenders had responded fast to the crisis, though. Linke was hot on Luke's heels now, while Tarnat was haring back to cover the middle. But Carl – Luke noticed out of the corner of his eye – had made a great run to Kahn's far post. Without even breaking step, he swung over a deliciously floating cross.

"Go Carly! Go Carly!"
roared the Albion travellers. The Pineapple Poacher arrived just at the right moment, leapt with the keeper, and got his head to it first. But his looping header wasn't quite on target.

Instead the ball plopped into the goalmouth mud and slowly trickled along the six-yard line...

Hold on – thought Luke, who was watching with bated breath – I've seen all this before. And he had! In the home tie against this same awesome opposition. The whole move was an almost eerie replica of Albion's best chance of the first half at Ash Acre. The one just before half-time – which Jimbo finished off by darting forward and doing the splits instead of scoring in an open goal.

This time, luckily, Jimbo was off the field. Not so luckily, however, the nearest player now to the bobbling ball wore a grey shirt with an *Opel* logo. Tarnat. And he had all the time in the world to trap it, turn, and hoof it away to safety. Or so Luke thought. So *everyone* thought. It was definitely what Tarnat himself thought. But that didn't take a certain Mr Dogan Mezir into account.

Beam me forward, Scotty, Albion's debut man could just have barked (if he'd been able to speak more than seven words of English). Just like before, he seemed to materialize from no-where. Moments earlier, he had been on the edge of his own box. Now he was on Kahn's six-yard line, *in front of* Tarnat, and, as calmly as you like, he was sidefooting into the net the goal that would take Albion past Bayern Munich into the quarter-final of the UEFA CUP!

Goal! *Goal! GOAL!*

No one had rehearsed this but, as the Dog wheeled away with one arm raised, all the Albion players – including Madman – rushed forward to meet him. Then, instead of just diving on him, they formed a line, grinned from ear to ear, and said with one voice: *"We are exceedingly pleased to meet you!"*

Then they dived on him, kissing and hugging him so hard that he must have wondered if he would get out alive. It was never like this on the lonely mountainsides of Armenia. Finally the ref broke up the party and the game went on. But not for long. The man in black didn't even take the whistle out of his mouth after the restart. Moments later he was blowing up for full time.

Albion were through! Their amazing quest for Euro-glory was still on!

The players rushed to where their fans were thickest, blew them all kisses, and did a victory dance with their fists held high.

"We Love You Albion,
Oh Yes We Do!"

Rocky and his backing singers boomed out in reply. Then they switched over to:

"We All Agree:
Castle Al-bee-yon Are Magic!"

before rounding things off by telling the lads down below that they were

"The Greatest TEAM
The World Has Ever SEEN!"

Gaffer then led his men back towards the tunnel. But just before they got there, Big Uschi came storming along the touchline towards them: face radiant with delight, arms flung out wide – and she was heading straight for Luke.

"No! *No!*" cried Benny, dashing forward and hauling his playmaking prodigy up and over his shoulder before she could steamroller him like poor old Jimbo.

"You were *wunderbar*, Luke!" the Headless Hero heard her cry as she came up and shook one of his dangling ankles. "Quite fabulous! The best player on the pitch by many miles!" Suddenly she burst into tears of pure joy. "Oh, Luke, Luke, Luke," she sobbed, "how does it feel to be so ... magnificent?"

"Pretty good, I'd say!" Luke heard as a hand ten times as strong grabbed his other ankle – Grandpa! "Your nan and I thought that parachute business would be the highlight of this trip. We've been wanting to do that ever since the end of World War Two! But seeing you out there tonight topped even that!"

"Cheers!" grinned Luke, twisting round. "I'll see you all later!"

"Yep, son, you did me proud tonight," born-again Benny agreed as he lugged Luke on down the tunnel, surrounded by the rest of the squad. " You *all* did. Every single one of you. On nights like these, you're just not the same side that gets tanked at home by the likes of Leek Town."

"But we're *not* the same side, are we?" whooped Half-Fat beside him. "Not with the Dog on board. No one's gonna stop us now!"

"Where *is* that Wonderful Woofer?" shouted Carl, looking around.

"There!" cried Dennis, pointing to the end of the tunnel, where Gary Newbon had collared him for a post-match interview. The rest of the players watched with broad grins all over their faces.

"Can you talk us through your second goal," Gary asked, shoving the microphone at the two-goal hero.

Dog shrugged, scratched his head, smiled, then said very clearly and very slowly: "I – am – exceedingly – pleased – to – meet – you."

The entire Albion squad burst out laughing – even Luke who was still up on Benny's shoulders. Meanwhile Terry was rubbing his hands with glee in the dressing-room doorway. "Well, that's Mission Accomplished, I reckon," he said, licking his lips. "A few German beers will go down *rather* nicely tonight."

"Beers?" snorted Benny. "You can forget about celebrating tonight, Terry. You and the Dog are going straight back on your bikes. We've got a tricky home fixture with Shrewsbury on Saturday – and I want Dog there in time for it."

Terry rolled his eyes. "Well," he sighed. "All

right. I'll get him up as far as Calais. But how am I gonna get him across the English Channel?"

"The way he played tonight," smiled Chrissie, "he probably cycles on water!"

"You could always hire a pedalo for the pair of you," suggested Craig.

"Or just get him to swim it," Madman put in. "You know – *Doggy* paddle!"

"You'll think of something, Tel, old son," said Benny, clapping his right-hand man on the back. "I know you will. You always do. And as for the rest of you wonderful *under*dogs – on this never-to-be-forgotten night in the roller-coaster story of Castle Albion FC, I've got just two words to say: *PARTY ON!*"